I0583116

Earned innocence

Copyright © 2017 C.M. Halstead

Cover layout by Timon Pratt, Studio 5

Edited by George Bass

Manufactured in the United States of America

For information, please contact:

C.M. Halstead

Copyright © <$2017> <$CMHalstead>

ISBN-13: 978-0-9863445-9-6
ISBN-13: 978-0-9863445-8-9
LCCN:
FICTION / Literary / Coming of Age / Military

1 2 3 4 5 6 7 8 9 10

Earned innocence

C.M. Halstead

To Those That Serve.

The most glorious job in the Marines,
is the guy that gets shot at.
Grunts, are what they affectionately call
themselves.

This is a story about one of those men,
put yourself in his shoes, for a bit.
Walk the walk, learn why he did,
and what he had to do to come home.

What would you do to regain your soul's
innocence?

The enemy is after my mind,
My mind is the enemy, and fear is his
name.
The enemy is after my mind, shame is his
name.
My mind is the enemy, I am he,
The enemy is not out there, the enemy is
me.

1

I walk out into the high desert, the intention to live the rest of my life there, laden with demons, my death shouldn't take very long. The knowledge that I won't be missed gives me a flexibility of schedule, I can live as long or as little as I desire. The desert welcomes me with bare arms, … it says to me.

"I guarantee to test you, dirty you, starve and dehydrate you. This is my promise and guarantee, whatever it takes to remove the demons from you, or kill you. Your choice!"

I hear this as I reach the edge of the tourist town that is Sedona, Arizona. My feet just shuffle on the sidewalk, scraping with resistance, the cars driving by alternate between the too-fast speeds of the local on commute and the too-slow crawl of the visitor seeking their hotel; lost by the local signage's proximity to the earth and the magnets that draw their tourist's eyes to the surreal monoliths of scarlet and cream sandstone. They ride their brakes, relentless in their distraction, the locals race around them. Knowing they will soon see them face to face across a counter, they keep their fingers, horns and comments to themselves. I hear both types of drivers, as I scan for the end of the sidewalk. "*It cannot come quick enough,*" I think out loud.

My cover pulled low on my head prevents eye contact with visitors and locals alike. A police car drives by at a steady rate, I feel the officer's eyes upon me. I likely appear as a hiker, walking out for his evening walk. Adorned in tan rip-stop BDU pants, light hikers on my feet, a long sleeve base layer, and a small backpack on my back, nothing about my appearance will say otherwise. The white cotton sunhat hides my features and dead eyes from him, a good thing, the silent challenge in them may have drawn the officer's attention. The police car continues to move on.

As my feet finally hit the red dirt at the end of the sidewalk, I lift my head with gratitude. The feeling of my boots digging into the sand as I push off and increase my pace, is just a natural reaction at this point. My muscle memory automatically triggering the training that started on the sands of Parris Island, South Carolina, the Marine Corp's east coast recruit depot.

Not all who desire to earn the title of Marine, are capable of doing so, and even of those that do earn the title, only about one quarter of them survive their full first term of enlistment. Many others, like me, even though they return home with all their body parts, still harbor the wounds of the job. Having stripped myself of the title that only I can remove from myself, I am grateful the desert will provide me a juxtaposed environment to decide if I can re-earn the title of U.S. Marine, or if it all ends here. My life, that is.

This is a good place to die, the desert will show my remains for decades to come. Showing all, my demise. In this case, I will not be forgotten; every javelina, coyote and turkey vulture that feeds upon me will be grateful for my death. As I decay over the years, the beetles, ants, and larvae will be the last to thrive off of my flesh, before keeling over of old age, a week or so later.

2

We slalomed between the short orange cones with nothing to lose, the suburban commuter-oriented, 4-door, American sedan creaked and groaned in protest, with each hard steering adjustment. We're on 490, a commuter highway in the "Can-of-Worms" area of Rochester, NY. Infamous for looking like a spilled can, that just a moment ago, was full of dark loam and fishing worms. Urban legend has it that the pilots of the traffic planes adorned the area with the nickname.

This highway area is an intersection filled with experienced Upstate N.Y. drivers, which translates to "Hold on to your steering wheel and make your move". Horns blast the area in communication and protest, regularly. A vehicle's horn is just an extension of one's mouth here. Beep, beep, for "Hey, I'm here," or "You go ahead," or just held down in anger, for as long as desired. Smiles usually formed in cars around the angered driver. We've all been there, no judgments made, no weapons drawn, it's not about me, after all. Just that New Yorker and whatever is going on in his/her life.

The Can-of-Worms area is eternally under

construction. I don't know if it's the long and brutal winters, forcing a continuous scraping of the roads resilient surface, against the onslaught of metal, pushed down upon it by a massive yellow truck, pushing with all its' might. Detroit diesel powered the drivetrain, forcing its' will against the snow from the early winter's lake effect snows, through the spring nor'easter's, snows measured in feet, not inches. During the winter seasons, cars that would normally be going 15 miles per hour over the speed limit, creep their way through the Can-of-Worms, at a speed slow enough to make the compacted snow and ice below their tires groan in protest.

The horns of half the year are absent, replaced by two hands on the wheel and super early turn signals. Everyone is still jockeying for position in their race home, albeit now, easing back and forward to keep a safe skid distance on all four corners of their vehicle. Light taps on the brakes let the person behind you know to reduce his urgency, or risk a lane change, while you grit your teeth and wait out the consequences of that driver's choice.

In the long winter season, potholes magically appear overnight! The tires bang down into them removing the contents, the plows come along and scrape it away, repeating the process, relentless in their mission to stay ahead of the snow and ice. Within hours, the newborn hole is big enough to lose a tire in its' depths. Now, however, is the other half of the year, construction season.

We've driven through this area several times, and know we're in the padding zone. New Yorkers are of the mindset that the road is two lanes, until it is not two lanes. In some areas of the United States, as soon as the merge signs appear flashing on the sides of the road, the drivers obligingly veer over into the lane the flashing arrow is instructing them move to. No continuance of travel, no using of the open part of the road.

Traffic backs up for miles, due to the over exuberance. There are even civilian law enforcement agents in their trucks and cars, that will donate their vehicle to the belief of adherence to the law of instant reaction to the flashers. They do this by moving over and obstructing others that don't follow their unwritten rule. We of Upstate N.Y., are not of that mindset; we're going to flow, right down to the end of the cone-induced devouring of the lane we are zooming along in. We may even move over into that lane to cover a little extra ground, if it is by some miracle free.

Brakes are applied at just the precise time, while the car is used to squeeze over into a magically appearing hole in the traffic. Because of this version of enthusiastic driving, there is an extended padded zone of cones, at most road construction sites. It is in this padded zone, the one that we have driven by several times in the last couple of days, that my buddy is maneuvering the car through. The tires screech in protest, and we laugh and giggle like schoolboys on a fun adventure. "What are they gonna do, send us to Marine Corps boot camp!" we cry.

Our impending departure is the reason we have been through this area many times as of late, but, with the final paperwork done, we leave for MEPS in two days. If they were smart, they would send us right now. Seeing the real construction area coming up, my buddy steers the vehicle into the open lane for good. "OK, now what?" we both exclaim. We have a party coming up tomorrow night, but tonight, everybody else is busy doing responsible stuff and shit. There must be something fun and mischievous we can do. "Hey, hey, I know!" he says.

"What? Whatcha got, man?" I'm excited to do something. The wake-up is beginning.

"They're changing the stoplights nearby Dad's house. Let's get the old one," he says.

"Wait, what?" I say.

"They're changing the stoplights; the old ones were on the side of the road when I drove by them yesterday," he says.

"Hmm, interesting," I say, "Let's check it out."

Intrigued, we drive by the area. The old stoplights are indeed, off to the side of the road, mostly hidden under a bunch of dark green tarps. Three of them lay dark and abandoned, their formal lights to shine no more. Dejected, they face their eyes to the ground in shame, replaced by four brand new, shiny, green and obnoxious lights, that surely can be seen from miles down the road, which is the Department of Transportation's intention, at this middle of nowhere intersection.

Produced to induce a driver-coma, removal and awareness announcement, they will pierce the night sky with sharp luminescent jabs of green, yellow and red, as required.

"Dude, they're enormous, we can't fit those in the trunk of this car, that's for sure," I say.

Looking at me, he says, "No shit Sherlock, I can get my hands on a pick-up truck...."

"Perfect. Tonight then?" I ask.

"I don't know. Let's get home and then I can make some phone calls," he says as he smiles mischievously.

We sit back from the intersection with a clean line of sight in all four directions. There is minimal traffic here this time of night, the light is really for the daytime traffic. Located in an area between the country, suburbia, and commercial work zones, it is an intersection of commuting for all that live in this rural area. At ten o'clock at night, most are home watching TV with their families, or drinking in the bars. In about 30 minutes, the barflies will head for their homes, and the sheriffs and state troopers will be abundant the roads. Our timing is perfect. One lonely pair of headlights makes its' way toward the intersection and we're waiting for its' arrival and departure. No other traffic is to be seen for at least two miles in the other three directions. As soon as these headlights make their way by, we will commence with our "commando raid", as we're thinking of it.

The two round beams emitting from the truck lights make their way to us and pass straight through the intersection. My buddy puts the pick-up truck into gear as we look at each other, and smile. We pull straight up the road and veer across, with no headlights to announce our actions; just the brake lights give away our presence, as he puts the truck into parking gear. Light bulb removed, the dome light fails to continue current and darkness prevails as we open our doors and walk up to the giant tarps covering the object of our desire.

"Shit, they're even bigger up close!" I say.

I see his teeth smiling bright, "Good thing we brought a tarp."

In the back of the pick-up truck, held under a couple of bricks, we have two old green plastic tarps, you know the kind, they're indestructible, until without notice, they dissolve into plastic threads, now as strong as wet paper.

These two are only about half way to that wet paper stage, and will hold up well, against the 60 mph winds of our journey.

Standing there, I can see enough of the three retired stoplights to know that they're all huge. There are two 4-way lights, and one 3-way, laying there, just waiting to be hauled away; perhaps their size is why they're still here in the first place.

We look at each other, "I don't think the two big ones'll fit. Maybe we should take the 3- way?"

We both look from the stoplights to the regular cab Toyota pickup behind us.

"It still won't fit," he says.

"I know."

"Where are we going to put it?" he says, rhetorically.

"I don't know, but, I think we should do it anyway," I say to him, looking for reaction. As the smile crosses his face, I have my answer.

"We can put it in my uncle's barn. Before he finds it, we'll be on Parris Island. What's he gonna do then?" he says.

"OK, let's go for it," I say, "It's going to stick way out, definitely need the tarps." I look up and down the roads, "Still all clear, let's go for it."

We make haste and pull on one of the tarps held down by local rocks. Pulling it back, we brace ourselves for the weight of the gigantic stoplight. It surprises us with its' lightness. Made of aluminum, or something else light and vigorous, it's easy for the two of us to lift. We hustle to the pickup and pitch the stoplight over the side and into the pickup truck bed. At first, trying to put two sides of the light into the bed and failing, we instead, put it in the bed of the truck at an angle, one side of the light full on the bed and another third, firmly placed on the side of it. We quickly lash it down, not bothering to keep an eye on the road anymore, for we are fully committed. Working quickly, we reposition the construction tarp back over the other lights and return the rocks to their holding-the-tarps-down position.

Leaping into our truck, we're giddy and adrenalized. He starts it up as I scope the road, "All clear!" I yell out to him, making him jump. Throwing it into gear, we zip across the east-west road and head south making our getaway. Laughing and feeling accomplished, we joke about what they would do if they caught us.

The Sheriff would say, *"You're doing what in two days?"*

"Going to Marine Corps boot camp!" we would say in unison.

"Get the hell out of here, there's nothing we can do to you then. They'll handle it," the Sheriff would say, as we leapt back into the truck.

"Good luck, you're gonna need it," he would say to us, as we do a burnout and pull away.

We have no idea how right he would've been.

3

Today starts the beginning of our second month. I know, so what? What does that mean? It means the Drill Instructors start to really turn it on.

We sit here, balancing buttons on the end of our rifles, small olive-drab buttons, made out of an almost indestructible plastic. If one were to attempt to bite the button in half, it would most surely break all his teeth, attempting the feat. This button, capable of surviving the apocalypse, was currently wavering, ever so slightly, on the end of my rifle. The rifle, pressed tight against my shoulder, is welded to my shoulder pocket. You know the one, the perfect place for the rifle butt to reside, where it will most likely stay in place, and when I graduate to bigger weapons; the only place to put the rifle end of anything resembling a big bore .50 caliber, or Enfield 303, anything like that. I could put those rifle butts in other areas if I chose to, I just might break a collar bone, or a rib, or an arm, is all. My choice, I suppose.

This rifle butt was nothing of that sort, in fact, quite the opposite. The M16A-2 service rifle, is a low recoil weapon. The choice placement of a fairly substantial spring, lessens the recoil of the quaint-sized 5.56mm round that is discharged from it; some say enough to fire a blank from the weapon, while held against your mouth, without even busting a lip. Obviously, don't try this at home folks, and never with a live round. After all, only a majority of Marines are well trained enough to pull off hitting a bullseye from 100 yards, with it held to their lips. Just kidding... maybe.

You may wonder if I drift off into daydreaming land frequently, and often? Yes, I do. It is the vain of my existence, especially back in high school. Who knew that, one day, this trick ability to check out and completely leave the building, mentally, would come in handy. Who knew that, one day, it would help my survival, and not just in the Marines, but, after.

That war, the after war, was way tougher.

It's hard to look back and justify a 17-year-old's way of thinking; it's nearly impossible, in fact. There's no way I can do that, at my current age, without putting experiences of the last 30 years into it. But, here it goes anyway: ....

I was totally and utterly bored with school, they did not manage to engage me or truly grab my attention. It is possible, that so many bad things had happened by the time I reached puberty, that I was beyond reach. I, however, remember a long period of boredom, starting from the time I woke up in the morning, to about the time I joined the military. Perhaps I was not made for a desk, or to sit still, and yet, here I sit, writing this.

So, let's go with the 17-year-old's memory of the school system, not finding the best way to grab my attention, and get me actually to give a shit, and apply myself beyond a "C" grade. I was one of these students that pissed off my friends, not because I was a dick, but, because I never did any homework, and I could just show up, and get a B+ or better, on the multiple guess exam. I could look at a math question, and more-often-then-not, figure out the answer in my head. The math teachers that got the best of me, are the ones that actually required us to show our work.

I was sometimes screwed on those. Imagine if I had actually done any of the homework, I would've managed way more than a "C" grade. Again, failure to engage….

So, and therefore, when most of those around me were discussing which colleges they were applying to and hoping to get in, talking about what their "preference list" was, I was thinking about what I could do besides continue on with an institution that had failed the last 13 years to gain my attention. I think I gave them a fair shake at it, it was time to try something different. I decided to do what most of the men in my lineage had done for the previous three generations, join the United States military. The only question that remained was: which one?

So, back to the button, the olive drab one we were just discussing. This button is still precariously placed and balanced near the front sight post of the rifle. My goal, for however long the Drill Instructors say, is to balance said button on the rifle barrel, taking aim by lining up the rear sight with the front sight post, while breathing, while placing my forward hand back onto the rifle (*from the multitude of times the button leapt to the floor, where it struck with a tight pinging sound, deadened by the realization that it is really just plastic*). Then, and only then, I pause my breath naturally, and slowly pull the trigger, 'til it clicks suddenly, releasing the firing pin forward to strike air, where a 5.56mm round will soon be.

The thing that amazes me the most is that, at that moment, just before the trigger goes, right as I pause my breath, my focus is becoming so complete that none of the sounds in the squad bay penetrate that focus. The moment I pull the trigger, however, all the sounds burst into my ear drums, the multitude of clicks from a room full of firing pins, and the constant sound of buttons hitting the floor blast my ears, as ear deadening as a rock concert.

Of course, and almost always, the loudest of the sounds in the barracks are the sounds coming from the quarter-deck. Those not acquainted with a quarter-deck might want to know the official definition of what it entails, and where its' location is on a ship, or in a squad bay.

Its' location is irrelevant at this moment and time; what truly matters is what the quarter-deck represents. I cannot accurately describe the experience that is recruit training at Parris Island, South Carolina, and leave out the place of wonderment that is, the quarter-deck.

For those of you that need to know what it looks like; it is a blank piece of concrete, located between the head (*showers and toilets*) and the DI hut (*their office and bunk*). This real estate is nothing but plain, unpainted concrete, that is regularly inundated with sweat, saliva, some puke, and a constant pounding of boots and hands. This is one of the places Marines are made.

Make sure when you arrive, at either Parris Island, or MCRD San Diego, that you tell each of your drill instructors, individually, and at different times in your training (*maybe from week three on*) that you are indeed, tired. Or, just be simple and leave out the indeed. Then you will get to experience what it is like to be truly worn out.!!! Of course, if you remember reading this, and think of telling your Drill Instructors you are tired and want to go home, then you'll be well acquainted enough with this quarter-deck, to be smart enough **NOT** to say that to them. And if you're a few weeks in and decide to inform them (*your DI's*) of your own physical state after reading this, then you're what is known in the Marines to be, a "*rock*". Don't worry, these rocks are sorely needed in the beloved corps.

I feel the Drill Instructor looking my way. Oh, shit! I had zoned off again and guess what, yes, that's right, he's looking right at me. Not with hatred or spite, just with that normal, I caught you, and now it's your turn, kind of look. He points his finger at me and gives me the come here curl, with said finger. "Gallaps, Jones, get up here also. You're up," the Drill Instructor says.

I get there as quickly as I can, careful not to walk in the middle of the squad bay, trip on my fellow recruits, or get taken out by any of them frantically lunging and grabbing for their own button. We form a perfect line, spaced just far enough apart not to hit each other, or get in each other's way. We know what is to come.

"Why you just standing there? Side-straddle-hops. Go!" he says.

We oblige him by jumping in the air, while moving our arms from our sides and clapping them over our heads, while simultaneously landing with our feet as far apart as possible, and still remain standing. "One, two, three ONE! One, two three, TWO! One, two, three, THREE!" we say as loud as one can, while attempting to breathe and exercise, at the same time. By this point in training, we're becoming pretty good at it, actually. Not quite to the latter stage, where I will be able to brush off a plethora of sand fleas, while doing these side-straddle-hops, without a DI even noticing. Regardless... "One, two, three, 38!"

"Push!" he says.

We get down to our toes and place our palms on the sweaty concrete floor, assuming a perfect push-up position, "One, two, three, ONE! One, two, three, TWO!" we shout. We're projecting our voices from our diaphragms as best we can, while accruing numbers of pushups. The DI looks at us over his shoulder, while he helps a recruit perfect his button balancing. He does this by placing the button steadily on the recruit's rifle, while said recruit is in the firing position. The Drill Instructor talks to him quietly, getting him to be calm.

He pulls the trigger, the button stays. From where I am on the quarter-deck, I can see the DI mouth "Outstanding" to the recruit, and smack him on the back, sending the button careening to the floor, it rolls away to land near another recruit's boot. Standing up, the DI pauses for a second, ...

"Mountain climbers," he says without looking. Waiting for the "Aye, Aye Sir!" from us recruits on the quarter-deck, before he walks over and with his boot, pushes the button back to its' current owner, simultaneously looking about the squad bay.

In the back, he catches a recruit picking his nose, "Are you kidding me recruit! ARE .... YOU .... KIDDING ME!?!? You're picking your nose!! You're really confident in your rifle skills, aren't you recruit!?!? You must be, to make your nose-picking a priority, during education time.

You must be so astute at it, that you would rather spend some time on the quarter-deck, with the other three. In fact, you're such an over-achiever, that I expect you to catch up!" He stares at the recruit as he hurries by, headed for his punishment zone.

A Drill Instructor's stare could melt a fish, yet, the recruit manages to keep his attention straight ahead. Not daring to look.

"You owe me 38 side-straddle-hops, 22 push-ups and…," he pauses to listen. We yell a little louder, "One, two, three, 40! One, two, three, 41!" by this time the other recruit arrived, and is pumping out side-straddle-hops as quickly as he can. "...41 mountain climbers, as well. Better get on it!"

We slow down our mountain climbers, ever so slightly. To be honest, by this point; our fatigue is creeping in, and we have no choice, but, to slow down. But, just a little. If we slow down too much, we'll never get off this quarter-deck. The recruit playing catch-up, is now pumping out pushups, and me? I'm about done with this mountain climber bullshit, and I'm hoping "the Heavy" doesn't keep us doing these until the nose picker next to me catches up.

"OK, as many pull-ups as you can and back to your rifles. Cheeks, Salazar, and Thin Man, get up there." The recruit that just joined us, up on the quarter-deck, gets up to join us on the pull-up bars; only two of them located on the wall, I luck out and get to wait a minute, while the other two crank out as many pull-ups as they can. He stands in wait beside me.

"Not you, Picker! You just got there; just for that, you owe me what they did, plus, what the new group is doing, as well." The offender gets back to his mountain climbers;

he will be up here for awhile. I finish my turn on the pull-up bar and head back to my rifle to recover, work on my day-dreaming, and practice the slow squeeze of the trigger, required to keep the bombproof button in its' precarious position on the rifle barrel.

4

My buddy from back home walks over to me, his back to
the DI on duty, he smiles at me and hands me the letter
from home that's in his hand, "Dude, you gotta read this!"
he says quietly. I, of course, take it, we will all read any
letter or outside mail of any kind handed to us. Any
insight into a world other than this one, is a welcome
break. Taking it, I see it is addressed to him, and at the
bottom, after a couple of handwritten paragraphs, it is
signed Uncle Donald.

Reading the letter: *"I am sure you are getting everything you
are looking for, out of boot-camp. I know they are getting more out of
you than you ever knew you had. At least, they did when I was there,
back in '68. They were churning and burning us through the system,
in order to send us to the suck known as Vietnam. You are lucky you
were able to volunteer for the green machine, while I was drafted, and
forced into it. Here's hoping they still kick your ass good, 'cause I
know you'll be sent somewhere to kick some ass."*

Next paragraph: *"Speaking of kicking some ass. I was doing
some spring cleaning in the barn the other day, rearranging the straw,*

sweeping out the mouse poop and looking through the various pieces of junk I like to hold onto, you know, that I pile in all the corners. Imagine my surprise, when I found, hidden under a tiny tarp in a little corner of the barn, a GIANT FUCKING STOPLIGHT.!!! Are you guys serious! When did you two little schmucks do this? It has to be you two, no one else copped to it, or has the balls to do it. So, here's hoping they drill you extra hard today, make you play in the pit more than usual, and when you two survive your tours of duty, I will hang the giant son of a bitch from the barn rafters and throw you a party. In the meantime, what do I do with it? Suggestions?"
Signed,
Uncle Donald.

Looking around, to make sure the DI is not in sight before speaking, I spot him busy digging some recruits on the quarter-deck, "Dude, that's awesome, and funny! We knew he would find it, but, I forgot all about it. Thanks for sharing, we'll have to take him up on that offer," I say.

Suddenly, we hear the voice from the ethers, "You two have time to talk?!? Get up here; we'll give you something else to do, since you're so bored," the Drill Instructor says. Damn we're busted. Worth it, just the same. I hand the letter back and head up to the quarter-deck again, for some character building. The thoughts of that fun night, a great distraction while I crank out some push-ups, mountain climbers, and bicycle kicks.

I look over at my buddy and see him focused, doing his best to keep the smile in his eyes off his face. Surely, he'll be punished for cracking a smile, all while he's being punished for cracking a smile. Even if he does get busted, I'm glad I will not be joining him in that extra punishment, well, chances are at least, that I won't be! If he and I had been honest with our Drill Instructors, then he and I would be punished as a unit.

You see, the Marine Corps has something they affectionately call, "the buddy system". We affectionately call it, "the buddy-fuck system". We did join up together, went to MEPS together, and traveled to Parris Island together. We did join utilizing this buddy system. It was pitched as an ally program, have someone you know from home with you, on Parris Island. Someone to help motivate you, and go through it all, together.

Luckily, while going through the in-processing that is MEPS, we heard that you should not tell the Drill Instructors if you did join up with someone else, because they will punish you together. Anytime I got in trouble, or my buddy got in trouble, we would be treated as one, and punished together. No way would we want to **do twice the punishments** we know training is infamous for! So, on pick up day, the day we first meet our trainers, when the Drill Instructors asked their new platoon if there was anyone here on the buddy system.

"They want to make sure to keep us together," they said to us. My buddy and I had already agreed to be silent and say nothing. Much later in training, almost at the end of our thirteen weeks of boot-camp, one of our Drill Instructors did find out, when he was asking everybody where they were from. He heard that my buddy and I were from the same town, he asked us straight out if we were there on the buddy system. Instead of being mad at us and punishing us, he just smiled and told us we were smart! We all knew that if they had found out sooner, we would have been triple punished for lying to them, but, at these late stages of our training, we were beyond all that, and

the DI's were becoming, at least partly, human.

5

This is one of those things that I knew was coming. It was in all the recruitment videos, and in the war stories, of all that have served. I often wondered how I would do on this day. Our entire platoon is lined up, the first man just ten yards away from an imposing rusty metal door, with hinges on the outside, and adorned with a giant sliding deadbolt. The rest of the platoon is lined up behind him in single file, at a perpendicular angle from it.

Being the lead platoon in the battalion, we're going first, per usual. Fine by me. I'd rather get it done, instead of standing around watching others go through it. Best to not know what is happening next, as of late.

Three Marines, in full MOP gear, walk toward the door and motion our DI to bring us forward. I notice our Senior Drill Instructor will be going in with us, as well. It's one of the reasons I joined, Marines lead by example. The door opens, our Senior DI counts us off and pats us on the shoulder, as we walk into the concrete block building, I hear a little tension in his voice, fuck, that is not good.

Gas mask on my face, I'm already sweating, blouse and trousers buttoned up tight and sleeves unrolled added to the tension and fear, while looking through that scratched, milky, lens of my gas mask. I'm surrounded by Darth Vaders, as the door goes closed. All I hear is heavy, stress-filled breathing. I see our Senior DI talking to our Heavy, just before he closes the door. A faint sound of sliding metal-on-metal, and then our Senior DI tests the door. It is locked tight, from the outside.

The Marine Corps is always up for some extra exercise, so we squeeze some in while the Biological Warfare instructors add **"CS"** gas tablets to a tin can, one after another, until I can barely see the recruits around me. Per new normal, I turn off my over-thinking brain, and just follow directions, best I can. First peel off of the gas mask is a feeling that will never be forgotten. I purge my lungs of the foulness, while regaining the seal on my gas mask. By the time I'm finished, only 4 breaths later, my face and the inside of my mask are covered in spittle and snot. And that's from just a taste. My nostrils still full of the skunk and pepper scent, the urge to cough is insurmountable.

After some more jumping jacks, we pull the mask completely off our faces, and with a hand on the recruit in front of us, do a lap around the room, and then, "Don and clear" our masks again, between moments of expelling items stored in the back of our sinuses, long ago. Thanks, I needed that out of there. I'm pretty sure I've been carrying it in there since I exited the womb. Somehow, there is a constant flow of that goo. I didn't know I had that much storage room in my entire head, to say nothing of just the sinus area.

The room fills with yelling and screaming; some of the screaming is Instructors, attempting to gain the attention of panicking recruits, and the rest is those panicking recruits themselves. Hearing a loud banging sound above the din, I gather my wits enough to see what's going on, the nosey bastard that I am, I want to know. I see through the haze. A huge, somehow still not entirely in shape recruit, is banging on the door. He, our version of the infamous Gomer Pile, is yelling for his mommy, and he's demanding to get out. "I want my mommy, I want my mommy, I want..." a Biological Warfare Instructor, or is it our Senior DI, tries to get the recruit's attention and calm him down. Instead, the recruit escalates, and after taking a few steps back, bangs his beefy shoulder against the door, and a second time, and a third. The door shudders loudly against the frame, and on the fourth blow, it flies open, sending the deadbolt, and our **Heavy**, who was leaning on the outside, flying. He flees the building expeditiously, screaming for his mommy, the entire way. The outside Drill Instructor goes after him, while our Senior DI closes the door and holds it closed.

See what I mean about going first? Imagine being outside, knowing you're coming in here next. Our final gas chamber torture, is to remove our masks and store them in their proper location in their pouch. It is not until each, and every one of us has those fucking impossible to snap, been around since World War One, metal snaps, snapped, that we're able to leave. Keep in mind, as I stand there with mine snapped, I have nothing to do, but, inspect my snot as it escapes and lands on the recruit in front of me, and my boots below me. Breathing as little as possible, I do my best, while watching the door through squinty eyes. I hack, dry and raspy, my lungs seeking mucus to eject the vile pepper-skunk mix from the body. I watch the door.

Eventually, it opens, and we exit, coughing and

spattering goodness around as we go. Walking us in circles to keep us occupied and out of shock while we recover, we watch the next group go in. At the very end of the line, I notice the big recruit that left early, heading in for more. He went in four times that day.

6

The DI steps out of his hut, letters and a few boxes in his hands. Mail call! Not wanting to get my hopes up, I work on remembering what day it is, when I hear my name, and again. I rush up, before he can say it a third time.

"That was close," he says to me, before holding the letter out in front of himself.

"Mail received, Sir!" I say, slapping my hands together around the letter at the same time. "Open it," he says, before releasing it to me.

Since the weekly letters from home are thick, and obviously not just a letter, I have to open it to show the DI, as do the two recruits who received packages today. More than likely, they will not be able to keep whatever is in the packages. If it's candy or food, it will be put into the contraband trunk until near graduation, when we will have a bonfire, and eat the entire contents at once. Impossible to fathom at this point, we all regularly have thoughts that the DI's are sitting in their hut, consuming the candy and sodas, regularly. Snickers and Ho Ho's surely devoured by the handfuls, at every opportunity. Every time they go in to change their clothes, another sweet is eaten, our imaginations tell us. Looking over at the trunk, I see it is filling, and know this is not the case, yet, the thoughts are still there. The projection is needed at times, in order to build a desire to prove them wrong.

Opening the letter, I pull out the contents and unfold the weekly Sunday funny papers for him to inspect. Holding the envelope upside down to show nothing inside, I also hold the flimsy newspaper at an angle, so that anything perceived to be inside of it would slide out.

"OK," he says, and dismisses me with a wave of his hand.

I make my way back to my rack, to stand next to it, and quickly read through the comics. Every week, my mom sends them to me. I'm not sure where the idea first came from; she's been sending these to me since about week two, I think. The first one arrived when my Heavy was doing mail call. He's the brute of the bunch, it's rare that I saw any nicety of any kind from him, especially at that point in the training. I just remember opening it and noticing what it was, before pulling it out, thinking there's no way I would be able to keep them, and being very surprised, and totally caught off guard by the arrival of Sunday comics, I made the mistake of making eye contact, and expressing my surprise.

"Don't eyeball me, boy. Show me," he orders.

I pull them out of the envelope and hold them out to him. Looking at them in disgust, he leaf's through all the pages and hands them back to me, "Go," is all he says. I stand there, frozen for a second. Maybe they are human, after all. "Go, GO, GO!!! Before I change my mind," I hear from behind me, as I get the fuck out of there.

Racing back to my rack and footlocker, I know not what

to do with my prize. It is truly a prize. Something from the outside world, that I get to keep, that may make me smile during my fleeting moments of down time. I walk in a small pacing circle for a couple of seconds, I can't sit on my bunk or footlocker to read them, so I stand between the racks, feet clamped together at the U.S.M.C. mandatory, 45 degree angle, and leaf through the pages of Family Circle, Bloom County, Calvin and Hobbes, all appear before me in full color. I search for it. Yes, there it is, the Far Side is there, in its' single square of satire. Staring at it incessantly, my bunk mate comes over and glances at what it is I'm doing. His eyes go wide with excitement. He points at his chest, meaning, *"Me Next!"* I nod my head in agreement.

The next week, another thick envelope appears, containing that Sunday's new comics, and the next, and the next. By the end of the second week, all six pages of the funny papers are being devoured and enjoyed, by the entire platoon. We'll take sanity any way we can, and the comics are perfect.

7

A new drill instructor has appeared today, to replace one that had mysteriously disappeared, a couple days ago. Rumor has it, that it has something to do with choking a recruit, after catching the recruit on a self-appointed head call. Read, going to the bathroom without permission. I know the recruit, and he probably deserved it. He's the same one that freaked out while in the cattle car, cried at night because of a toothache, and, well, the list just goes on.

I know we all are hitting various physical and emotional bottoms, we all have our horrible days by design, but, when the moments of self-pity and failures start to add up, it's the recruit himself, who's starting to stand out, also part of the training. Weeding out the problem children ahead of time, saves drama in battle, there's enough of that, without having Marines calling for their mamas, instead of the Corpsman. Regardless, we can't have that now, can we? We can't have the Drill Instructors choking their recruits because they defied them, by using the head without permission. So, the Drill Instructor was transferred to another platoon in our series, and today a new one arrives for our platoon.

The one who just transferred out was a young Sergeant. He was cool, a younger guy, blond cropped hair, always had a chaw in his mouth. His replacement is the complete opposite; a Gunnery Sergeant with a patch of graying hair on his head, cropped high and tight. He smells like cigarettes and bad coffee, he stands all of 5' 8", and is slight of build, as most Marines are. It is obvious to my eyes, that he's in good shape and ready to go. With more time in than the last DI, he has a lot more years of Marine Corps in him. No introductions are made, no formal announcements, like on pick-up-day. (*The day we first met our Drill Instructors*). Nothing. Never the less, he quickly made his own impression on me, and the other recruits.

The day after Gunnery Sergeant Pazorski magically appeared, he found himself alone with us for the first time. He had us all lined up on "*the line*". The line ran the length of the recruit area of the squad bay; it was created by the application of white paint to the cement, starting at the edge of the quarterdeck and running from stanchion to stanchion, the entire length of the squad bay, ending at the back wall. That white line, created an area for us to put our toes, and also created a no-recruit-area in the middle section of the squad bay, that the Drill Instructors patrolled, relentlessly.

The line is also where we stood for inspections, to present items, during "Mount Iwo Jima", or while playing "water fountain," or just plain ol' standing there, while the DI's do whatever it is they do, when they leave us standing there at attention. On this day, the new Drill Instructor was getting us, used to **him**, his personality and his methods. Training the dogs to obey him. Out in the world, this takes a power struggle or, at least, an establishment of boundaries. At this stage of boot camp, for most of us, the fact that he is a Drill Instructor, is enough.

Cheeks, a recruit from the Island of Manhattan, 144th Street to be exact, was in a mood, and had been for a couple of days. Perhaps he's wondering if all this bullshit is worth it. He's been grumpy, and a "dinkus" to his fellow recruits for about a week, unusual for his personality. He's usually one of my fellow invisible ones, those of us that manage to stay off the radar of the DI's, more often than not. That's actually a skill in itself. A survival skill I learned in dealing with my step-dad. Today, when Drill Instructor, Gy/Sgt Pazorski walks by, inspecting each of us briefly, and finding something to attend to on each of us, in the half a second he looks our way, Cheeks just basically tells him to "fuck off".

Gy/Sgt Pazorski walks by each recruit and says something. "Blouse half tucked in, boot untied, belt undone, you have two different socks on." Stuff like that. I know, I know, we're adults right, and based on the above, you would think we're a bunch of kids, right? But, what I have left out is, we had just gotten done with a long period of being messed with, by several of our DI's.

This included dressing and undressing several times, and also dumping the contents of our sea bags and footlockers in a giant pile, in the middle of the squad bay. That, and rapidly retrieving them, in an ever-reduced time frame, designed for failure, in order to instill the belief of never being good enough, never fast enough, in us. A game lovingly called "Mount Iwo Jima." The rest of the Drill Instructors had walked into their DI hut, to do whatever it is they do, and left the new guy to help us sort ourselves out.

When Gy/Sgt Pazorski walks by recruit Cheeks, he says, "Tie your boot," and keeps walking to the next recruit. It takes a millisecond, and then Gy/Sgt Pazorski leaps backward, and puts the brim of his DI cover into Cheeks' forehead.

"What did you say, recruit?" he asks Cheeks.

"No," recruit Cheeks replies, again. Bewilderment fills the squad bay.

"No? Did you say no, recruit?"

Recruit Cheeks looks down at the Drill Instructor standing below him. You see, Recruit Cheeks stands about 6 foot tall, and has the type of physique that required others to scratch his back for him. His arms are pumped up tight, his biceps bulging, laterals creating wings on his back, and pectorals that rival the Incredible Hulk's, when he's on a rampage. Cheeks stands there, a mere two inches taller than the DI, but, about four times wider. None of it fat. Recruit Cheeks showed up to Parris Island, cut, and put together like a body builder. If you're looking for a cover photo of a Marine, he's your guy, a dark black man with a wide flat nose, he is a quiet presence. Not one to rebel or cause trouble, he seems to work at being invisible, my constant goal, as well. Cheeks and I get along, not that anyone here gets to hang out and chat about the old days. I do know that he's from Harlem, and he's one of the biggest, blackest, most cut, humans I've ever met. Quiet as a bear, he goes about his thing with humbleness and focus. He will be a good Marine, if he makes it.

Gy/Sgt Pazorski stands below him, with confidence and rage, glaring up at this recruit's defiance.

"I told you to tie your boot recruit, do it now!" he

commands the recruit, in his truest combat voice, confidence and grit flying from his mouth in the form of spittle and coffee breath.

"No," recruit Cheeks says again, this time removing his hands from their place on the seam of his pants, he attempts to push Gy/Sgt Pazorski with both his giant hands.

"Fuck you!" Cheeks says, looking down at Gunnery Sergeant Pazorski. Cheeks looks him right in the eye, keeping all other military bearings, whether he knows it or not. Gunny doesn't flinch.

The giant recruit choosing this moment and time, to challenge everything the Marine Corps stands for, doesn't faze him at all. It is his job, after all, to push, and push, and push, 'til each man faces his fears, demons, and stands up to the oppressor.

"You sure about that recruit.?!" This was more of a statement, not a question.

Today, today Cheeks has had enough; today is his day. We all have ours here; some have lots, today it is Cheeks. Or least, this moment is. The Drill Instructor stands there, unflinching, looking up at the giant of a man.

Cheeks, being one of the biggest members in our platoon, it may come clear to you now, how I'm connected to him. This 200 pounder, is one of my fireman's carry buddies, and constant opponent in the line program, and other hand-to-hand combat training. One of the first things I noticed about him, is he always works more on his technique, than trying to hurt me.   There are a couple here that try to take their aggressions and frustrations out on this little guy.   And those, those I make pay.

"Well..." Gy/Sgt Pazorski says. Cheeks flashes, and with

both hands, pushes at the DI. ***BAAM!*** It took like, a millisecond. Maybe a tad longer. Recruit Cheeks is flat on his back. Stunned, he lays there for a second. Wondering what happened, he reaches up to his face, bleeding from it just a little bit. I cannot attest to exactly how he got there, just that he did, quickly and effortlessly. Cheeks expelled zero energy, yet, managed to fly from his position on the line, to the concrete, with a brief blur of motion that was Gy/Sgt Pazorski, putting the man in his place. Not with hatred at the recruit's standing up to him, just that it was his job. It is his job to challenge, and push, and put into place, as necessary.

With no effort at all, that little old Marine had the bodybuilder on the floor, staring up in disbelief, at the ceiling above him. The sound of a thunderclap filled the room, followed by a startled gasp, drawn in through the noses of 50 or so recruits, standing and watching through their peripherals. No one challenged Gy/Sgt Pazorski again.

Cheeks gets up, rubbing his jaw and walks back to his normal position on the line, is perfectly lined up between two other recruits, and he stands at attention, staring straight ahead. Conflict over, we move on. Somehow, in that instant, that little old dude, magically teleports the recruit from his standing position, to one on his back.

"Now, where were we?" Gy/Sgt Pazorski asks, to no one in particular.

From the DI hut, we hear, "Head call and then classroom time."

"You heard the man. Move, move, MOVE," stepping into the middle of the squad bay, Gy/Sgt Pazorski watches the recruits make haste to the head, where all 60 of them will have about two minutes to do whatever needs to be done. He has proven his point; no other recruits will challenge him. His 8th day here, and his reputation is solid.

8

At the end of every PT session, is a glorious 3-5 mile run. Nothing better to work out the kinks, after an hour or two of calisthenics, obstacle courses, and a circuit course, not to mention a plethora of other physical strengthening activities.

Being of very slight stature, the runs are of no consequence to my knees, or my energy levels. I can coast around in the middle of the pack, and unseen, recover some energy for one of the day's activities that did tax me greatly; these types of activities include: heavy packs, the fireman's carry drills, and any other activity that will require me to carry my body weight, or more. Every time we practice carry drills, I am required to carry the biggest members of our platoon. Being one of the smallest, this only makes sense. Wouldn't it suck to get shot, and have this tiny-ass Marine come running up to you with intentions to carry you somewhere safe, and have him look at you and go, *"Shit, sorry dog, you're just too big for me to carry."* No! You would want him to grab your shot-up-ass and carry you back to Doc, or the chopper, or anything other than leave you there. It's why we join the Marines after all, isn't it? One of the reasons I chose to, at least, never to be left behind again.

The biggest guys in our platoon ranged around 200 pounds, I range around 120 pounds when full of banana's and ready to step on the scale! The first couple of times I picked one of these guys up, it was brutal. I think my lungs are going to burst, and it feels like my bones are working really hard at not crushing, and my knees... my knees drive themselves down towards the earth, desiring greatly, to make contact with the dirt. I refuse! I ensure I have a great carry position, I gather them up and I lift with all my will, standing tall as possible with them strewn across my back, one arm between their draped legs, I grasp their far arm for support, looking at my target destination, and off I go! Not running, for that would end my legs, yet, fast and steady, I make eyes for the end, both rifles in my left hand, I go, go, go, 'til I am done. That's all it takes, simply the will to go, go, go 'til it is done!

So, the runs... the runs are recovery time. At least, until Gy/Sgt Pazorski arrives, that is. It took him a week or so, but, he figured out that I like to hang out in the middle front of the group, and coast my way through the run. Not in the front, and not in the back, way ahead of the curve, yet, still not applying myself to all out speed, by any means.

Suddenly, startling me from my thoughts, "What the hell are you doing recruit? What are you doing here, you should be in the front!" he says to me, appearing next to me and running effortlessly, kinda like me, except **he is running backwards**, so he can give me his DI death stare.

"I smoked sir!" I reply, "Smoked till I got off the plane,

sir!"

"Bull," he says.

"No sir, I do... did!" I insist.

"I don't care, that's the sorriest excuse I've ever heard, you coasting maggot. Get your ass to the front, were you belong. I smoke. I smoke a lot. Heck, I'm smoking now, you lout.   MOVE!!!" Gy/Sgt Pazorski says to me, **while still running backwards**. "Get moving," he commands.

Spinning around as I apply some speed, he chases me to the front of the pack, astutely informing me of how many cigarettes he has consumed on a daily basis, for as long as he can remember. All the while, chewing my ear off, while running at my heels, just outside of my foot planting zone, he leans in for effect, until I reach the front, then slows down to find another recruit to harass and educate.

My days of coasting in the middle of the pack are over. I now must apply myself on every run, ensuring I no longer catch his eye.

9

Recon school isn't about being the biggest, the strongest, the fastest. It's about being forced beyond the breaking point, and not breaking anyway. It's about treading water until you drown, and getting back into the pool again.

The longest three miles of my life, were at the end of this school. It's during that crucible that I solidified in my brain; I am the secret to my success, I decide whether I succeed or fail, but, I get ahead of myself here. We aren't going to spend a lot of time on specific schools, lengths of time spent at each, etc. The principles of the ones that I remember, most are the same. A positive mental attitude is key to survival… so, let's see if we can get you to quit on yourself. Might as well know now!

Selection in Special Training

One of the first things I learned about survival, I learned before I arrived at Parris Island, Camp Lejeune, or Camp Pendleton: Shutting off the brain helps. Shutting off the brain is key. Thinking too much, is the death of your will.

I'm still treading water, who knows how long it has been, I checked out mentally a while ago and stopped looking at the clock. The bastards hung a huge clock behind them, with giant black numbers. At times, the ticking of the clock's second hand can be heard above the din in the pool. Keeping my head tilted back, I alternate my arms and legs in circular motions, as I've been doing for what seems like hours now. In order to keep us fresh, the trainers mix it up a bit. Here, pass this weight around, hold it for the count of 15, and pass it on to the next guy, all while treading water, …. ok, just your hands now, …. just your legs now, …. hold a rifle over your head, while singing the Marine Hymn. The list goes on.

I have my brain effectively shut off. Taking the pain is easier, when I don't think about it. My legs and arms had long ago gone numb, from cold and exertion. I am cold and shivering, as I look up at the sky and watch the clouds go by, that one looks like a frog, that one a cloud, that one a rabbit, the suns shines cool through that one, this one is darker than the last one. I continue my self-imposed distraction techniques, as I move my legs and arms, per the last order.

Whenever they change the order, I'm forced to break my trance and listen, and watch. I am to the point where I have to really focus, to comprehend what they're now instructing us to do. It's in the beginning of one of these changes in focus, that my body shuts down. I move my eyes from checking out animal formations in the clouds, to the Marine standing on the concrete edge of the pool, trying to push me over the edge, so I will quit. Looking there, I see a man not much older than me, and as slight of build, standing there shouting more instructions to the Marines in the pool, working on convincing their bodies and minds not to quit.

I'm watching him, seeing his mouth move, yet, not comprehending what he's saying, I try and focus, he gets blurry, and taller suddenly. I see a figure dive into the pool off to my right. Turning to see who he's diving after this time, my body lowers itself into the pool. This milky figure works its' way over to me, as I fade to the bottom of the pool, my body arches backwards, and I get to see what the clouds look like through about 10 feet of the pool's water.

"What am I doing down here? I'm supposed to be at the surface." I tell my body to get there.

My body doesn't respond to the order, I decide maybe I need to go to sleep, or maybe it just happens. I wait for impact with the bottom of the pool, so I can rest in peace.

"He coming back." I hear with closed eyes. I feel the cold pool concrete on my back. Thinking I'm still napping on the bottom of the pool, I keep my eyes closed for a few moments more. It is then, that I feel the breeze going across my body on fire. Everything tingles, I feel every single one of my pores standing at attention, the hairs working hard at escaping into the ethers, I wonder what is going on, a shadow goes by, blocking the sun.

"Get out of my sun, you fucker!" goes through my brain. I feel myself shiver, more of a shudder, actually. The fucker is still standing in my sun, I open my eyes to see who it is.

"Welcome back, Marine." I hear from the shadow. I will my entire arm to raise from the cold concrete and motion for him to move. My hand, from the wrist up, responds. It flaps back and forth like a fish on the shore.

I see him look at my hand and then the shadow he's

45

creating over me. He moves, the sun graces my face. I smile and close my eyes, as I turn to the sun a little more. Feeling the topside of my water-cooled body warm just a tad in the sun, I lay there with a smile across my face. Closing my eyes, I listen to what is being said nearby.

"What do you think Doc? Is he good to go? Do we need to drop him?" the voice says.

"Let's give him a minute," another voice responds.

Drop me? **FuUUUck you!!!!** Opening my eyes, I look around to see what's going on. As is par for the course today, there are a couple of us lying on our backs, I look toward the pool, everybody that is left, is still treading water at the moment, with rifles held over their heads. I see two Marines nearby, they're the ones talking about me. Looking to the left, I see the Marine closest to me, squared down at my level, paying attention to one other candidate, who's still unconscious, yet, breathing.

Looking back at the pool, I see they're handing most of the rifles in, one Marine is now instructed to keep one. It's time to pass it around, butt-to-barrel, butt-to-barrel, it will be passed around. Now is my shot, they will not decide for me, if I'm able to continue. I move quick. Before they realize it, I enter the pool. I slip in, sliding with my best otter impersonation.

"Hey!" I hear behind me. "Come back here, Marine!"

"He isn't cleared," I hear Doc say.

Fuck you guys, I say to myself. I'm not finished yet, you'll have to come get me. I don't challenge them to, because I know they'll enter the pool to get me. Instead, I ignore them and slip all the way into the water. I feel a hand grab at my blouse and I shirk it off quickly and violently. Swimming over quickly, and clumsily, I move into the circle, and I'm let in without hesitation, by the remaining Marines in the water. When the rifle comes to me I grab it and pass it on, to the next Marine.

"I'm staying bitches," I say out loud, to no-one, but, the Marines in the pool.

"Oorah." "Semper Fi." These are the responses I hear from them.

Even some mild laughter, from two true bad-asses who haven't seemed fazed by a single thing, and saw me escape back into the pool.

"There's your answer," I hear from Master Chief behind me, "Leave him be," he says to the other decision makers.

Relinquished from control of my fate, the Marines move on to deal with the next Marine making his choices while laying on the concrete poolside, belly up, facing the partly cloudy sky, no conscious thoughts that they, in that moment, are deciding their fate for the next few years, and maybe forever.

In the pool, we keep up our games for what feels like a few more minutes and then are told to get out of the pool. Smart enough not to believe this day is over, I'm still joy-filled, that we're probably done with the pool, at least for today.

Getting out, I stand there shivering for a moment, the Marine that was squatting down between me and the other Marine walks by and pauses to get in my face for a moment. His face is glaring and stern, his eyes are smiling and proud. He looks from me to another Marine being escorted out to join the other 20 or so Marines that either quit today, or were dropped for some medicals. He looks back at me, speaking nothing. He says everything with the look in his eyes. I look at him for the first time, and realize he is the little Marine that was upfront giving orders, when I went to the bottom that last time. He walks away....

I stand there shivering and exhausted beyond description, proud I will make it now. This is the only part I was worried about. I fucking hate water. If we humans were supposed to be in it, we would have gills, not lungs. I hate it, I hate it, I hate it. I will do it again if need be, every time.

I think, but, I'm not sure, I think, I went down three times today. Do not ask me to testify, because the brain makes everything worse than it actually is. Hard to believe on days like these.

"CONFIDENCE IS SOMETHING A MAN
EXPERIENCES, JUST BEFORE HE LEARNS ALL
THE FACTS"

10

Three miles is all we had to cover. On an average day, a group of Marines will take about 30-40 minutes to cover that distance, depending on combat load and terrain, faster, if in a hurry. This day? This day it took about three hours, an hour a mile. Not bad, all things considered.

The gas hits us, I see it coming toward us again, and again, always at just the perfect angle, riding the wind into our formation. Well, actually, that formation simply disintegrated, in about five minutes. From then on, it turned into a cluster-fuck. Damn trainers, why do they have to be so good at what they do?

We've been at this for awhile now. Most of today's mission has been routine to all other trials and tribulation training, as I affectionately call them, "this Marine has been shot, your wagon wheel fell off, get this barrel over the pool of water… Oh, and your right arm just got blown off, good luck! Here's your map, now you can either climb up the cliff face, by hand, or go five miles around." Shit like that kind of training scenarios.

So today, when a couple of the trainer Marines smiled, when M/Sgt laid out the final task (the crux, the crucible, the mighty motherfucker, whatever you want to call it), I knew we were doomed. Three miles back to base, carry wounded and fallen, got it. Wait... that's just too easy.

When we're training, the Marine Corps doesn't save the easy mission for last, not in any of the training I participated in, at least. Quite the opposite, actually.

M/Sgt himself, laid out the first few gas canisters, he and some of his cronies (I have lots of worse comments flowing through my head about them at this moment). Three or four "CS" gas grenades are activated, about 20 yards ahead of us, upwind, and in a perfect location to be blown across the road that we're making progress on.

It's my turn with the dummy, representing my fallen buddy. The 180 pound dummy, combined with the Alice pack and its' contents, drive through my body toward the ground, my shoulders drag as I walk forward, leaning into the hill. I close my eyes as the wave of gas hits, I take a step, four inches is how far my foot moves before it hits me. Keeping my eyes closed, and my breath held, I take another step. I'm not going to breath yet, I take a few short whiffs through my nostrils, my lungs are bursting and burning from lack of oxygen producing energy, as I test inhale the smoke.

Having done this before, I have a pretty good idea what's going to happen. I fight the panic, just a few small teases of its' nastiness reach the spongy parts of my lung's breathing apparatus, and it's already affecting me. I take a few more steps. I'm in the thick of the smoke now. Doubled over pretty far, from the weight on my shoulders, I find my face searching for the ground. Leaning just a little too much, the ground zooms in for a close-up. At the last second, I realize I'm headed for a hard face-plant.

Managing to tuck my head at the last second, I bash the corner of my forehead and my shoulder into the ground. The poor plastic bastard that I'm carrying on my shoulders, takes most of the blow. A moment ago, he was laying across my shoulders, in the classic combat carry. But, when I went down, his right "leg" along with my elbow and forehead, took most of the impact.

A slow-moving boot catches the back of me, pitching forward onto me. Thankfully, that Marine rolls forwards, off me. One of the other Marines, who's currently unencumbered by objects and comrades, trips over me. Looking up, I see another Marine let go of him, he was trying to lead the men carrying our "package" through the smoke.

My eyes apply crazy glue to the tops and bottoms of their eyelids. Forcing them to do their job of keeping out the jalapeño-filled smoke, while they demand the brain send all the body's water to them, to rinse the eyes from the inside out.

Sgt. Crabtree leans down and helps me up. We stand there with our eyes mostly closed, adjusting the wounded man into position, so he can be re-applied to my tired shoulders. "Let me take him," Sgt. Crabtree croaks.

I shake my head, "It's still my turn, if I give him up, we may have to do this again." Shaking my head is making me dizzy, although it takes a bit to figure that out, so, in this state, I keep shaking my head until it sinks in.

He smiles at me, "Fuck that," he mouths, and we put my burden back on my shoulders. I start taking steps again. By this time, most of the smoke has cleared out of the area. After a few more yards and moments in time (miles, years even), I'm told to release my marine to someone else. I'm granted a few burden-free yards. I stand up for a moment, stretching out my back, my resilient 19-year-old body feeling lots of pain and soreness. None of it old, all of it from the last few weeks. All it takes is a day off, and my body is ready for more. Not sure when I last had one of those. Tomorrow.

Just as the burning soreness is leaving my shoulder muscles, it's my turn to help with the Rolling Contraption of Doom. I can't remember what condition it started in, now, it's a barely rolling mess of unattached wheels, something that looks like fence posts, and a lot of rope. I move around and push from the backside. We're dragging this burden, more than rolling it along. I start to yell a suggestion and a mouthful of "CS" gas enters my mouth and finds the path to my lungs. Before I can do anything, I start coughing like crazy, and everything that is in my sinuses plunges rapidly for my boots. I sneeze. Mucus, and various other fluids, leave my face and redistribute in multiple areas of my uniform, boots, and the apparatus we're moving.

Suddenly, I'm now hyper-vigilant about the amount of snot and various other liquids that are covering the logs, wheels, rims, and anything else we've been leaning over. My hands are covered in this nastiness. I snort out another bucket of slime from my nose, it hangs from me to the ground. I keep moving my feet, pushing with what little might my gas-infused muscles have. My boots slipping on snot, every step a double step, the phrase "two for one special" goes through my brain. The opposite is reality, though.

I put my head up and look ahead of me. Marines are struggling all around me. Coughing. Sporting tears from gas and possibly frustration. Growls, groans, anger, screams at themselves, their recruiters, the trainers, the person that "voluntold" them to be here, can be heard through the chaos. All these sounds enter the background of my being, as I take another step and push, another step and push, another step and push. From now, until they tell us to stop. All of us are suffering and moving. Puking is allowed, as long as, we don't stop to do it. Keep moving forward. When one goes down, we help him up. Progress is being made.

Somehow, in this moment, I flash back to boot camp. Now a lifetime ago, the memory is vivid in my head. I remember pushing myself, really hard, after our DI, Gy/Sgt Pazorski gave me that pep talk, during a run. The next couple weeks I pushed myself to run as fast as I could, and to keep up, and then catch up, to the 17 minute runners. Recruits that are the fastest in the 3-mile run section of the PFT's, are a barometer for the rest of us, and our level of running fitness.

These guy's times range close to 17 minutes. At that point, I had not yet learned to lengthen my stride. Although I have long skinny legs, I was taking the short steps learned from formation running. I worked my body into an exhaustion a few times, before finding a way to ask one of the quicker runners what I was doing wrong, why couldn't I keep up? His reply was simple, "Take longer steps, lengthen your strides, you look like a midget running, but, you have a three foot leg length."

What led to me being desperate enough to risk communication with a recruit (we didn't exactly sit around and chat) was puking for like a week straight, during those PT runs we had at the end of our physical training sessions. The second time I paused to puke during a run, my Senior DI gave me the ol', "What are you doing? Keep running. I said keep running." Once I did start running again, he says, "It's OK to puke, puke all you want. Just keep running, don't stop." By this point in training, I knew the DI's aren't joking when they say stuff like this.

"OK, let's see if we can muster some kind of formation Marines!" our M/Sgt yells at us. The voice removes me from my thoughts. I had retreated there, to escape the pain and agony of the day. Looking up, I see he and the other trainers, standing side by side. M/Sgt and the other instructors, although still in a condition better than us, are not sporting their "normal" perfect appearance. Sweaty, dirty, and feeling some effects of an inherent inhalation or two of the "CS" gas. GOOD.!!!

They muster us in a formation and we manage to adjust arms; just turning my head and then raising my arm to adjust positioning, is an act of god. I have no idea how my arm raised when I told it to. I fight back tears of pain, and joy. I did it. I_fucking_did_it.!! Nah, this was just selection, and not everybody that makes it this far gets selected, and not all that get selected, can make it through the next segment of training, or their complete tour. Not able to think about that right now, all I can do is bring my arm down and snap-to, with all the confidence and energy of the Marines before me. I see pride in M/Sgt's eyes. Real pride. His tears may be from the "CS" gas, but, then again....... I'm starting to figure out these guys, and their mindset, the brutal training is for a reason. After all, if anybody could do it, it wouldn't be the Marines.

"The more we bleed, in training, the less we bleed, in war. Don't let this become a cliché' for you, Marines," he says. "This is the last test in the selection process. You men standing before me, have passed this test." M/Sgt looks us up and down, searching for each Marine's eye. Well, most, some he avoids. He does look at me. Instantly filled with pride, I work hard at not getting worked up. I never think I'm good enough to pass, yet, my reviews always tell me that I kick ass. What's that about, I wonder? Who's lying to who? "We will let you know tomorrow, if you've been selected! Enjoy your evening. Dismissed!" M/Sgt turns away, hands behind his back, and waits for his trainers. They walk away talking enthusiastically. I'm sure they're already making up their final decisions, or just as likely, telling war stories from the day.

Sgt. Crabtree is standing to my side, waiting for me to come back from my too frequent daydreaming. As I turn, I see him standing there. "Dude..." he says, as we clasp hands in glorious congratulations. Not able to muster much more enthusiasm than that, we chat, as we limp back to barracks, within a couple hundred yards, we gain the ability to walk a semi-normal gait, although we have the "I just climbed a mountain, or day hiked a rim-to-river-to-rim in the Grand Canyon"-type of hitch in our step. We walk tall and straight.

We have grandiose plans for the night: Marlboro reds, Skoal classic, and beer, are our desired rewards for the evening. Even later in the evening, jokes about women and getting laid will be in effect. Right now, a hero's welcome and victory sex are off the table. Even I, would not fuck myself in this condition; dirt, sand, twigs, and grass, are in every crack and crevice of my body and uniform. Every time I go to wipe my nose, I am reminded of the "CS" gas that embalmed itself into my blouse top. About mid-wipe, the gas kicks in the flow of boogers again. This process will continue until I'm in the shower, for sure. I smell like sweat, earth, and other Marine's mucous, and amazingly, I even smell like urine. Pretty sure, I did not pee my pants today, though. The salt and sand scrape madly at my legs, arms, and anything that moves.

During the walk back, my body seems to feel everything it had shut out over the last few hours.

Pebbles of sand in my boots turn into boulders, each grain of sand on my blouse and pants, race to scrape their mark into my skin, razor blades by the thousands.

"Let's go straight for the shower," I suggest.

He smiles at me, "Good idea today. We don't have to do the test, we know our cami's would stand tall today."

I smile back, "Field shower!"

Stopping at our racks, we dump the packs and a few beat-to-shit items from our pockets, some of them unidentifiable, onto our racks for cleaning and redistribution. Wanting to beat the rush, we decide to police up items, and do the gear exchange later. Walking into the showers, we see we managed to beat the rush, there's just one naked Marine, and two others already doing what Sgt. Crabtree and I were about to do.

We head to the back corner and standing next to each other, turn both knobs on half way. The water is freezing at first, but, at least, I'm awake. It warms up pretty quickly, since the other men already had the hot water flowing. I put my face in, straight up at the blast, feeling the dirt leaving my face, and after a few seconds I breath better, the "CS" gas remnants off my face. I tuck my head forward, so water can run the gunk off my head as well, the dead muskrat living on my head, surely holding more sand and dirt than the outdoors, at the moment. Opening my eyes, I watch the dirt leave my head and swirl around in the water, inter-mingling in streams with the whirlpool below, it finds its' way into the drain. Grass and mud slide off me and my uniform, quickly clogging up the drain, I move it off to the side with my boot.

Looking to my left, I see Sgt. Crabtree in a similar position, making eye contact we laugh at the absurdity of the day, and giddy at the prospect of actually becoming, Recon Marines. The best of the best, unarguably. Just ask them and they'll show you. Talk is cheap.

Laughter is about all we can get to escape our lips, even the talkative bravado he usually spews is non-existent. If we end up in separate parts of the fleet, I will miss this mid-western s.o.b., the image of him talking smack with a big ol' chaw in the left cheek, will always be in my mind. A mere 5' 8", his stocky presence likes to hold court for several audience members, every chance he gets. He thrives as a live storyteller.

Getting lost in my own world, I reflect on the last few weeks, the last few hours locked away somewhere else for the moment. I reflect on me and my fellow Marines' actions and our responses to the training. It's hard to know how I, or anybody else, will react to a situation, until it is done. The beauty to me, of going through all this hell at such a young age is, well, I'm young and old at the same time. Older and wiser than most my age, I will realize that soon enough.

At the moment, I focus on getting me and my BDU's clean. Unbuttoning the top button I pull the blouse off over my head. Turning it inside out, I rinse off the dirt and sweat and I notice blood on the right side of it.

Looking down, I see it on my t-shirt, as well. That's mine. Gingerly, I lift my shirt and see a gash, and a huge bruise forming. Hmm, who knows when I did that? I sure as hell don't!

Finishing my blouse, I follow the same process with my t-shirt and work my upper body until it is clean. Unable to stand and remove my boots per usual, I sit down with my feet in the water and remove the jungle boots one at a time, rinsing one completely, before moving on to the other, inside and out. I see one of the lace eyelets is busted out. I may have to fix that.

Double layers of socks come next, the filth that comes out of them is amazing. Rinsing feet and toes carefully, I work between all the toes, mindful not to pop any of the blisters in the shower. I will handle those on my rack in a short bit, with my field sewing kit, Neosporin, and maybe even some Moleskin. My feet finally clean, I remove my pants while sitting, having just watched Sgt. Crabtree fall over in the effort of removing them while standing. I fuck with him about why he keeps this young guy around.

"Yet another reason, why I have more wisdom than you," I say to him.

Laughing he says, "Fuck you. You're just wise enough to watch others try it first, and learn from their mistakes."

"Exactly!" I say.

Standing up slowly, now just in my tighty-not-so-whities, I remove them carefully, as to not become the butt of my own joke. Dirt and nastiness found its' way all the way down to my crotch; cleaning it out of there and my butt crack, brings me to the welcome conclusion of my shower. The shower room is filling up at this point and I grab my gear and make room for the Marines waiting in various states of dress, some naked, carrying all their clothes, others like Sgt. Crabtree and me, are starting their showers completely clothed. Walking with all the grace of a wounded, one-legged giraffe, I find my way back to my rack and treat my wounds.

There's a Navy Corpsman working the squad bay, as well, doing his best to make sure no Marines are hiding serious injuries. He checks each man off his list, after having a conversation with him and inspecting their body. He makes his way over to me, "Hey Doc, what's up?" I say.

"Gotta check you out Marine," he says.

"I didn't know you were into that kinda thing," I reply.

"Don't ask, don't tell, remember," he says, smiling. "Anything I need to know about?"

"Um, just maybe my ribs Doc, other than that, I can handle the blisters," I reply.

"Well, let me at least see the blisters." He checks them out and decides to help me with a deep, bottom of the foot blister that I hadn't even noticed yet. Buried in my heel bottom, it would have been really hard to deal with.

"Anytime you get these, make sure you pop them. They can get really big and next thing you know, your whole heel callus peels off," he says, looking at me. "Not joking! So, FYI. Now, let me see those ribs."

I stand and turn so he can have easier access and lifting my arm, I expose the bruised and scraped area. He applies massive amount of orange nastiness known as iodine, and cleanses the area. None of the scratches are deep, but, the risk of infection and cellulitis is high in our line of work. Doc pushes with his hand around the rib area. None of the pain is unbearable.

60

"They're probably OK. Might want to have 'em x-rayed, after tomorrow," he says. Doc is smart enough to know, none of us will be visiting the medical center today, unless we're forced to, at gunpoint; nothing to increase a possible risk of one NOT being selected now, is allowed at this point.

"OK Doc, thank you. I'll see how they feel in the morning, OK?" I ask.

"Well, if you can't sleep from the pain, then definitely get them looked at."

"An elephant could probably walk on me tonight, and I'd sleep," I reply.

He smacks me hard on the shoulder a couple times and says, "I bet Marine. Good job!" and moves on to the next guy.

After policing up our gear and ensuring we have the required amounts of everything, Sgt. Crabtree and I head off to grab as much chow as our bodies will keep down. Afterward, we head back to the squad bay. There's some bravado going on there, but, not much. Most are exhausted, a few are worried, and a few are sitting around joking about each other's lows from that day. It's a great sign of brotherhood, when you can joke with each other about your limitations and failures.

So far, most of the training I've done in the Marine Corps has been about trying to break me and my will. I look forward to some straight up education. Believe me, I never thought I would say that. Laying on my rack face down, I push my folded pillow out of the way and pass out, on top of my wool blanket.

11

Reveille wakes me up the next morning. I lift my head from a pile of wet drool, reminding me of yesterday's fun. Today is Selection Day.

After chow, we all head to the classroom to await our fate. The air is heavy with anxious anticipation. The fear smell is prominent in the room, and the instructors do nothing to lessen this feeling. They talk to none of us, lest we figure out, one way or another, if we've made it.

At exactly 0900 the meeting starts. Running the meeting in the typical Marine fashion, they get right into it. After a short speech about effort, and not all make it, and they can try again (*imagine doing this twice! Easier, or harder, the next time?*), we then are informed that some names will be called. About seven or eight names are called, and they leave the room with a few instructors. M/Sgt and a few others gather in the front, whispering to themselves, leaving us to sweat in the silence.

Unceremoniously, M/Sgt turns around and says, "Congratulations Marines, you have all survived the selection process. The Marines that got called from the room did not, they will be informed of their options for returning to the fleet, and the possibilities of giving it another go. You will now start the next stage of your training...."

I made it! Really, again! How is it I keep slipping through the cracks.?.!.? Surely one of those that got called away is better than me. I run through those Marines in my head. OK, no, they all had a few obvious *"oopses"*. Hell, we all had *"oopses"*. After all, it's not about failure, it's about how we handle each failure that matters. How many times do I get up? One more time than I've been knocked down, that's how many.

The hard part is over, I made it.

12

Gy/Sgt Pazorski sits me down. Somehow, I'm ending up in his own unit. I say somehow, but, like I said earlier, Gunny's been stalking me since boot camp. I don't know if this is how it always works, but, it's how it's working with him and me. Reminds me of growing up a military brat.

Every one to three years, we had a family meeting and found out where we were moving to next. It depended on everything out of my control as a child, us children had no say. Dad, as he gained rank, had more and more say. And we moved to further and further locales, as he and mom desired to see things they wouldn't otherwise be able to see, at the government's expense. We would move from one far corner of America to Europe, and then back, a few years later.

The amazing thing is, as we got resettled into our new base housing, segregated by enlisted, officer, and rank, within those two categories, we would often run into someone we knew, from a couple bases back. They, flowing along on their own military-induced gypsy life, also moving according to their own and the military's desires, would cause our paths to cross again. Strange enough, just because your family was tight with them a few years ago, doesn't mean the two families will be tight now, at this base and time. Ranks change and a lot of us took each move as an opportunity to reinvent ourselves. Therefore, we could change personalities, habits, and favorite activities drastically, within a few years. No one I knew ever took this change personally, none that I know of at least, and if they did, I sure didn't.

So, perhaps this is how it works with Gy/Sgt Pazorski and me. Perhaps not as well, the amateur philosopher that I am, likes to think that life is deeper than that. I do need someone like him to teach me what it's all about. Positive role models are not prominent in my life, prior to him. He's one of the reasons I joined up.

"You're young, really young, for what we do," he says to me.

"All of us are young Gunny, the oldest guy in my platoon in boot, was 27, and they called him the old man! Aren't we all young?" I ask of him.

"Yes, but, some are younger than others," he says, grinning. "Most that come into these units, are experienced elsewhere. Usually from combat, or growing up in the projects, or barrio, or something," Gunny says.

"I have seen death," I said. "I first saw death at six. Watched my brother get run over and killed, by a contractor trying to find a house one summer morning. Having a late start to his day, he decided to hit the bar for a couple hours first. A choice that ended with an image of my brother and the bicycle he was on, rolling around his right rear tire, forever imprinted in my brain."

"I'm sorry," he says. "I didn't know you lost a brother."

"I did, and I watched it, too," I say, "Lost my innocence

that day."

"You will lose more," he says, "You will watch men who are becoming your brothers, die. Strangers, too. People you have no idea of their story. Those images will join those of your brother's."

"I know," I say.

"You will not be on the news, you will not be paraded, and we will not talk about what happens out there, with anyone other than one who was there when it happened, and even then, not so much," he says.

I laugh. "I know, Gunny. This may actually be easier to take, than straight combat. Such is the story I tell myself, at least," I say, looking at him.

He smiles. "Don't know if that's true or not. I do know, I saw the right tendencies in you, pretty quick. Not one to draw attention himself, instead, quietly kicking ass and leading, once I woke you up from skate mode, your safety mode, that is."

He looks at me through his eyebrows. "Then you started excelling, instead of just skating by. Your scores were already great, and jumped higher, and so did your skill set. I was tempted to try and grab you into this, without going to the school, but, figured it would do you good, if you survived it." He grins ear to ear. "That school was a fucker, wasn't it?"

"Yes, yes it was. Is the Marine Corps done trying to break me, Gunny? I'm getting tired of having all my buttons pushed constantly. It gets old," I say.

"It does, doesn't it? Well, you're with me, I know your buttons and how to push 'em when necessary, if I want to. Other than that, you've passed my test, young man. I can't speak for the other team members, though, you'll still have some proving to do with them. Especially with your lack of combat experience, rank, and the fact that you look like you're a freshman in high school," he laughs again at that. "As soon as they saw you, they started calling you "the Kid." I'd get used to that, if I were you. Worse comes to worse, you can just start acting like Billy the Kid, although that may get you killed. Oh, yeah, and that reminds me of my rule #1, on each and every mission."

"What's that?" I ask

"Don't get dead," he says.

Gunny gets close, he comes into my space in DI mode, and wags his finger, "Rule #1, each and every time. Always remember this, when facing an enemy: It may be honorable to die for your country, but, its' better to make some other motherfucker die for his. You hear me?"

"Deal, Gunnery Sergeant," I say.

He grabs me and puts me into a headlock as he starts walking, "Good, now come meet the rest of the team. Oh, yeah, another surprise, your buddy is also joining us, as well, Sgt. Crabtree."

I smile and try to talk through friendly brutality of the lock.

"Awesome, just awesome!" I croak.

13

I hold my breath and put my hands in the air. Arms held out slightly to the sides I watch the hand-held metal detector with my peripheral vision. The Marine operating it has one eye on its' path, and the other on the recruits all around him. It is his, and one other instructor's, job, to make sure not one live round or bullet casing is removed from the rifle range. He moves the black plastic device down the length of my right arm and across to the tip of the left one.

A few moments ago, I had a brief conversation with my buddy. "Dude, you didn't bring the watch, did you?" he says to me.

"I did!" I say, a little panic in my voice. Right now, it resides in its' normal place, my pants pocket. The watch has endured and survived everything Parris Island has thrown at it. I can still remember the moment I pulled it out of my blue "contraband bag". Way back in the receiving, about 4,000 years ago, they had us gather all our valuables that we would not need during our stay here at the resort known as MCRD, Parris Island. We put them all into a small blue plastic mesh bag, a white cotton string to hold the contents tight and secure. Then Drill Instructors, in their infinite wisdom, decided to let us keep them securely locked in our foot-lockers.

The sneaky s.o.b. that I am, on more than one occasion, loosened the draw string to look into the bag at the cheap gold chains, heavy ID bracelet, the waterproof Casio watch, some coins, a pen, and a thick leather wallet. A few dollars float around in there, as well. I remember reaching in to hold the watch in my hand, and looking at the digital numbers, wondering if the time is correct. Looking up at the squad bay clock, I see it is still stuck on 2 minutes to 12. Fuckers....

On that day, I reached my other hand inside my footlocker and into the blue bag, I took the rubber watchband tight in the hand and wrenched the band back and forth, forcing it to torque until the watch-pin broke free of its' assigned position. I then did the same to the other side of the watch band, holding the watch face in my hand for just a second. After contemplating the consequences of my actions, I pulled it out and put it in my pocket. I knew that some of the classrooms we go to have clocks on the walls, and I would be able to check it then. It would be totally and eternally awesome, to know what time it is. Just being able to look at it once or twice a day, would be a great victory. This went on for a while.

Soon, those closest to me learned about the watch, and when it was safe, we managed to look at it and tell each other what time it was, and we theorized what we would be doing next. It has been a great distraction.

At this moment, standing there with my buddy quickly adjusting our BDU's and squaring ourselves away, as an excuse to stand there and figure something out. We have a few seconds to do it quick.

"How about your boot, they have a metal shank in them?" he says.

"Too obvious," I say. Tucking in my olive drab t-shirt, my hand catches on the belt buckle as I tuck. Hmm, why not, I can just tighten it a bit. The skinny recruit that I am, they won't be surprised if it looks like I am trying extra hard to hold my pants up.

"I got it," I said.

"Tell me," he requests.

"No time. Later," I reply.

We're already attracting attention from the Marines standing about 20 yards away from us, with metal detectors in their hands. Always on the watch for recruit shenanigans, they're surely wondering what we're talking about, during this very rare opportunity. It's cool of them to not give us flak, yet, we know if they find the watch, they will.

Placing the watch in the area between my belt and pants, I cinch the belt slightly, forming a strong bond between the three objects, and walk forward, confidently. It will be a small price to pay, if they do find it. At least, it's not a bullet, to pull a "Gomer" with.

The Marine works his way across my chest and down each leg, working closely through the boot area, I now know he would have discovered anything not located at the bottom of the boot, I hold my breath for the final pass around my groin area. The detector does its' thing when it reaches my scratched up belt buckle, by screeching its' pleasure at its' discovery of metal in two spots. The marine waves the device around the area, scoping it out in detail. He pauses it, directly in front of the buckle, and follows it slightly to the side, to the location of the end cap of the web belt. The tiny piece of brass at the end squeaks its' presence. The marine backs away and motions for me to go. I double-time away, willing the watch to stay. Hurried into formation, I have no time to relocate the watch back to my pocket. It will have to endure the trip to the chow hall. If it falls, I'll just play dumb.

"Dude that was close!" my buddy says, as he catches up to me.

"I know, I know!" is all I can think of saying. Inside, I'm feeling glorious, I got something by these guys. It truly is a win!

Little did I know that watch would spend the rest of boot camp in that position, tightly held behind my belt, sans the wrist strap. The belt location is an easier spot to scope out, when the desire of time to be known, arrives. No reaching into the pocket necessary, hands in the pocket are an alarm call to any Drill Instructor. One of the best ways to grab the voracious attention of any and all Drill Instructors on the planet, current and former, would be placing your hands in your pockets. Marines don't walk around with their hands in their pockets.

Gunny Pazorki laughs, "That's a great story, Marine. I like it. Especially that you got one over on me. None of us had any idea. You have to know by the end of boot camp, there are always some things we know about and let you recruits get away with. Sometimes we even let things go on a bit at night, if you know what I mean?" he says, knowing that I do know exactly what he means, referring to the infamous, yet rare, blanket parties. Soap, socks, and a wool blanket, were the tools of late night discipline. It was more about your platoon having had enough of your shit, to give up a little bit of their precious sleep time, to let you know that you were a fuck-up, than the pain of a soap-filled-sock hitting your body. So says someone who was never on the receiving end.

My turn to laugh, "I do Gunny, I do! How about you, did you get away with something you shouldn't have, especially while in boot?"

"That was a long time ago," he says, "But, yes, I do remember a few things. Like skating on runs, until my Heavy came up on me and put the fear of god in me. He followed me and harassed me on every run for the next two weeks, until I just automatically started running like I was trying to outrun my heals. There've been times I've had to run like that, so, I'm glad he did it!" Gy/Sgt Pazorski finishes the statement with a laugh.

14

Motley Crüe blares on, throughout the helicopter, small speakers located on the deck between the two pilots is the source. Being that this was my first "green" mission, I was given the honor of choosing the motivational music. Resisting the urge to pay homage to the famous 'Apocalypse Now' scene, I instead, chose the music of high school. I heard tell it has been used to instill fear in Panama, and me, I just love it. Kind of worked on the parents a little bit, as well.

I steal a glance towards Gy/Sgt. Pazorski, "Do what I say and you'll be fine, don't and you are dead, maybe..." was about all he said. Then he smiled and flashed those shiny white teeth. The guy must have an addiction to peroxide or something, to keep his teeth that white, with all the cigarettes he smokes. It's amazing how they almost glowed in the dark, when I watched him painting up.

Through the speakers blares the song, harsh and tinny, *"Shout, shout, shout at the devil."*

Ironically, at my high school, some kid that might possibly be a devil worshiper, actually killed a teenage girl and her baby. There were always lots of rumors and shit about headless cats they found just outside of town, and don't go up that certain hill on full moon nights. Hell, that hill was creepy every night, big old concrete water towers loomed over by trees, and modern day stilted round towers with views of the town, if you could earn it by climbing the ladder. After the murder case, we all started playing Motley Crüe's 'Shout at the Devil' song at the home basketball games, and it was amazing how much it charged us up, knowing it was demoralizing the visiting teams. The tension caused by the recent memories of those events was obvious. It was intimidation at its' best.

I lean against the bulkhead and breath deep, smelling some sweat and fear (*probably mine*), CLP, camo grease paint, exhaust and fresh air, all blending together. The music blares and I'm grateful for the choice in music. I cannot believe I signed up for this shit, well, kinda. What did they see in me, that made them think I was made for this, or am I still cannon fodder, just a little more trained? I wonder if the other Marines in the helicopter have these thoughts. Am I the only one? Does one having these thoughts make me a newbie, do they make me weak, or does feeling, make me strong?

There's nothing like the sound of guitar riffs at full blast. The sound interrupts those thoughts and brings me into the music. I'm charging up from the music's energy and thoughts. Gunny Pazorski having to listen to Motley Crüe is a bonus.

It's amazing how everybody is in their own little world, every Marine getting ready in their own specific way. I wondered if any of these guys were superstitious, I know some long-timers have specific rituals, and others seemed to not really pay attention, or give a fuck. They're hard chargers, and this is just another day in the office.

The song is fading out, I look outside, seems I can barely see tree tops as they breeze by below me in the dark, nary a C-hair separates us, is how it appears to me. Looking to the front of the helicopter, I wonder what it looks like through the goggles the pilot's wearing, and wonder if he would be this close without them. Probably even closer.... I hear tell of brushing the trees and bouncing off the ground at times, when touch downs aren't even on the agenda.

Hell I don't care, if these guys are ballzy enough to do this all the time, they must know what they're doing, they've succeeded thus far, and their lives are also on the line if they fuck up. I'll just chill and enjoy the ride.

There's something amazing about the almost-being-able-to-float and go anywhere, turn-on-a-dime capabilities, of these strange contraptions. Almost defy the laws of physics, these big ol' helicopters do. Must be why they don't crash too well. The pilot and his crew will perform about five "landings" tonight. We'll participate in an unknown number ourselves and at some point, I'll find out which stop is ours. The others are just fakes, so if someone does happen to be in the neighborhood, they just think we're crazy, or if they're in the know, they'll have a hard time figuring out the game plan, and during which touchdown we departed the chopper. For not all of our chopper dismounts are from a land-based chopper, many times we speed rope, or rappel.

Hell, I don't even know the game plan for this part of the mission, I have enough to worry about.

I don't mean the "**am I tough enough?**" stuff, or "**what if something happens?**", but, will I keep my shit while it's happening, my bearing, not be a stupid motherfucker and f-it up, and get someone killed, or force us to go loud, or just... that kinda' shit. The pilot comes on over the speaker, interrupting my constant brain flow, "This one's yours," he monotones, informing us our cab has brought us to our destination.

The doorman splays out the rope, we gather up and ready ourselves. Corporal Alvarez grins and says, "Remember, if the mutha fucka below you fucks up, just plant your boots on him, squarely, and do your thing, he's the non-hacker, no reason you should break your legs!"

"Whatever," Sgt. Crabtree rebuts, since he is going just before me.

Speed roping from a moving vehicle, while hovering above the ground, is something brave and stupid enough that Marines love to do it. If you let go, you're fucked, if the guys below you dog pile, it's gonna hurt. And it's gonna hurt a few miles from home, with a mission still to accomplish.

"Reaaaaddeee!" I shuffle up a bit more, I'm going third, Gunny behind me, and Sgt. Crabtree in front of me, obviously second. I stifle a puke. Damn stomach, they're just starting to use this DNA shit, and I'm paranoid as fuck about it, leaving my DNA somewhere to be found is something I am not fond of. Fuck, I think too much... and like they'd have that sort of technology out here anyway, but, hey, we would wouldn't we.?.

Gunny's and Joan Jett's song comes on, just before we make the commitment, *"...it's all the same, somewhere take you home, where we can be alone, me, yeah, me…"*

"Let's go!" I hear Gunny yell, over the din of the chopper, Cpl. Alvarez, myself and Sgt. Crabtree, go in an

instant. I feel Gunny above me, or maybe it's just that all familiar rush from reaching out of a hovering aircraft and dropping into gravity, hands grabbing, feet find a purchase, slight spin, yep, I remembered gloves, kinda feeling.

I look down, Cpl. Alvarez is off and moving, Sgt. Crabtree hits and rolls and then, *bammm*, it's my turn. I roll and take my spot, adrenaline almost blinding me, just how am I supposed to see my sector, if I'm fucking blind? Relax Marine! I tell myself. I feel Gunny hit behind me. Then the last two Marines. The rope pulls up the instant it's free of the last Marine. The chopper and its' crew are off to do a few more mock drop-off's, and keep 'em guessing.

I hit silent mode in my mind.

We wait, … nothing.

We wait, … still nothing.

We move, we wait, … still nothing. We make eye contact with each other, ensuring all are accounted for and injury free. We're all good to go, no injuries from the speed rope dismount.

Gy/Sgt Pazorski sets us moving in the right direction, off to some cover to wait in. My eyes adjust to the dim light over the waiting period. It takes about 20 minutes for even our trained eyes to fully adjust to the dark. In the meantime, we listen to, more than watch what's going on around us. No human sounds are heard. This is my first time in a jungle-type environment, and I'm amazed at how truly accurate people's description of the night-time noise is.

Howler monkeys do their thing in the distance, mosquitos horde themselves around us, buzzing as one, they sound like a motorcycle of the rice-rocket kind, infinite in their high-pitched buzz. The overall din of the insects and night-callers turn into normal background noise within 20 minutes there. It will only be on a rare occasion, over the next hours, that I'll actually hear them. Although if they ever go silent, I had better hear that.

Chance of someone being at our LZ is slim to none, we're so far from our site objective and any other "known" live locations. They've given us a good one…., our mission, that is, full of speed moving, and distance to cover, before we were to possibly see something. Something I sure as hell don't want to see, and if it's a true event, I want to see about stopping it, and fucking them crazy bitches up. Oh, wait, we're "green", green as any Marine can be, there's no fucking it up, just swift, silent, and deadly. If they're done, nobody hears it. Preferably no one is done, and no one knows we were ever here, because we weren't. Aren't probably supposed to be, and I truly wonder where we are, that we aren't supposed to be. Besides surrounded by mosquitos, that is.

I couldn't help but wonder for a moment, what the rich people are doing, the high school senior, the old fuck sitting on the park bench, checking out the 'young' 40-year-old woman, and wondering if he can last long enough to make her orgasm a few times a week. Me? I'm sitting here in the damp, clammy air, feeling the moisture of the ground through BDU's, glad I have my favorite boots on. I wriggled my toes, and then I stretched them out on the ground, first the left, then the right, shifting my stance, Gunny looks over at me, fuck!

Narrowing his eyes and focus, he looks through me and then motions to Sgt. Crabtree and Cpl. Alvarez to head in my direction. Apparently, we're heading behind me, slightly up a ravine that leads to a partial notch and up a slope that has a few more slopes above it.

Like I said, they've given us a good one: 10 kilometers before morning, in the dark. Gotta' love it. And I do. The night is perfect, the pace will be fast, but, sustainable. Cpl. Alvarez will be up on point, looking here and there, always moving and looking. We're traversing a ridge now, about halfway across, with a long flat stretch ahead of us. It seems like a gamble to me, to hike so close to a ridge-line, but, I have to think those Military Intelligence guys know what they're doing, right? Gy/Sgt. Pazorski, I think, has a similar feeling, because he's slowly moving us off ridge-line, now that we're off the narrow patch, heading down the west side of the ridge, even though we're headed to the east side, for our final accommodations of the night. Surely, a dense patch of jungle growth, with great views of something spectacular. Good sight-lines all around, and nary a breeze to carry our scent, or any little *"oopses"* of wrappers, smelly contraband like chew, hard candy, unlit cigars (no-one would imagine smoking anything out here). Although, at this point, I'm chewing tobacco heavy, while on night duty, or fire watch. Nothing better to keep me alert and steady, than nasty tobacco in my lip, creating a slightly numbing sensation on my lips, and a slight buzz from the nicotine. Plus, if I do start to fall asleep, the lack of spitting causes a drowning sensation that will ensue, which startles me awake, keeping me and others alive.

Moving through an area that you don't know, at a rapid and quiet rate, can be a challenge, and it's probably why we've spent so much time practicing it. I almost feel more comfortable, walking around at night, than during the day.

We move swift, and with utmost silence, until we reach our destination. Once there, we will settle in and wait.

The scene unfolding down the hill, is something no one should see, ever, but, now it is my turn to see it. Old beat-to-shit military surplus 'deuce and a half' trucks come lumbering into our view; armed men and women spill out of the fronts and backs of them. Soldiers, ones that had gotten there earlier to set up, come out of the jungles surrounding the battered clearing. They gather in their conversation, smoking and chatting aimlessly. Nonchalant in their demeanor.

My senses are up, I look over at Gunny, he's looking down at the happenings, I try to read his face, impossible. He feels me looking and slightly turns his head and eyes me... hard. Using his eyes, he gets me to hand him **'the set',** the phone receiver that's attached to my radio. I reach back and turn the dial as low as it can go and still be able to hear those on the other end. The last thing I want, is for those below, or anyone on patrol in the area, to hear. It's amazing how far unnatural sounds carry, when they're the only sounds around. Imagine, if you will, the sounds of a red tail hawk, as it's flying through a quiet business meeting, ... you get the drift.

Gunny's getting no luck with the radio. Not surprised, am I. Glancing around, I'm greeted with faint light, highly filtered by the dense canopy above.

Not much in the way of sight-lines, or open area above us, the radio signal is probably getting lost, just bouncing among the giant tree trunks and pizza-slice-sized leaves. Someday, I'll have to come back to this area and check it out. A surreal quiet engulfs the volumes of bugs, birds, and monkeys, thickly scattered throughout this jungle. I feel Sgt. Cowan looking at me, intensely at that. Fuck, was I day-dreaming again? A good way to die.

I look toward Sgt. Cowan and he has a finger on his lips. Somebody must be coming, I look toward Gunny, he's already handing me the handset, and worming himself silently back into the darkness of his spot. I'm shrinking into the ground's shadows, as well. Tipping my boonie cover slightly, I get a better angle at the view around me, without the intensity of my eyes showing. Even completely camouflaged and hidden, it is still a good idea to never look hard at anybody, we're not the only trained people on the planet. It's amazing how, if you're aware, you can feel someone's gaze, or glare, or hot look of affection (*my favorite*) from afar. Even while you're distracted on something else, in fact easier when relaxed, and allowing it all to flow.

Then I hear them, two sets of footsteps, soft on the damp soil. They're coming from just under the ridge-line, using its' cover. Smart, hopefully just told to, not knowing to do that. Two coming our way, one male, one female. Evenly spaced, about three paces apart, they walk in a relaxed fashion, slowly glancing up and down the ridge-line. Pretty casual, but still, all very business. They've done this before. I quickly wonder if I would hesitate, if I had to kill this woman. Then I wonder if she would do the same for me. Hesitate, that is.

The breeze is heading in my direction and I start to smell them, they smell the same as the jungle, but, with a little hint of food and spice added in, and definitely some tobacco and pot, as well. Suddenly, I tried to imagine what it would be like to be here and high on something, talk about day-dreaming. Gunny would definitely love me then!

I keep my eyes low. The two walking guards will come to within 15 feet of us, if they continue their current path; always a little freaky. I focus on controlling my fear. I don't want them to smell me, when they get down wind of us. There is nothing more smell-able, and nothing better to set off a predator's alarm, than the smell of fear. *"Come to dinner, come get me,"* is what it tells our senses. Dinner is over there, ready and hiding. You just have to scare it out of hiding... you can smell its' fear! Time to devour it…, feed off the fear.

The rotten smell of the earth gets sharper, as my senses go on high alert. They're getting closer. I can now make out details of their clothes, they're wearing a strange combination of military surplus. It seems to be gathered from both cold war camps, some American, and some communist block. The guy appears to be wearing the same type jungle boots as me. I wonder if he's my size? They walk right by, mindless of our existence, lost in their conversation and flirtation with each other.

Action in the clearing below, draws my attention away from the two on patrol.

CLAANG, the first rear gate to one of the trucks bangs down. Then another, and another. ***Claang. Claang.*** The sight of soldiers reaching up into the backs of these trucks, has an ominous air about it. I see a little old lady being helped, commandingly, out of the back of the military surplus truck.

She wears a skirt of multiple bright colors, her shawl also consists of many colors, as does her loose-fitting shirt. Each of the three clothing items, consist of very different patterns, clashing together, peacefully. She's followed by a young mother, with a baby wrapped in a shawl and held firm to her breast. Several men follow, dressed in old button up cotton shirts and jeans. The armed ones help the human contents remove themselves from the military trucks. People of all ages are assisted to the ground.

Women, men, and children, start growing in numbers in the clearing below. Within minutes, an entire village appears, young, old, and everything in between. They all look the same from here. Those that are armed, and those that are not, seem to have similar heritage. Catching my bearing, just before letting out a deep sigh, I glance around at the Marines around me. Expressions change slightly, as it sinks in. Never having seen it before, I lie to myself for a bit, attempt to, at least. The situation becomes apparent, 20 or so armed personnel, probably six or so patrolling, and about 200 innocents, enough to create a village. A stern premonition voice in my head reminds me of the emphasis to not go loud.

Going loud is almost always considered a failure, so emphasizing it, seems redundant. What do I know though? This is my first mission this deep! Thinking back, I remember there were actually a few other Units at the pre-mission briefing, that means there are a few teams out here, scouting possibles, and we're the ones that hit the jackpot. I hope we are, at least. No one else needs to watch this.

I reach back to grab the handset and stretching, I hand it to Gunny. He grabs it without looking, I think he's counting the number of civilians milling about down below. He makes a call home, I absentmindedly reach over and adjust the knobs, check them, at least.

Quite the racket is developing below, the sounds of anger and confusion hurry up the hill to us. It seems the unarmed ones are not happy and are putting up a fuss. The herding begins. Those men and women and perhaps teenagers with the weapons, grouping the others in tight circles. Men, women, children, and babies are packed tight, creating a multi-generational mosh pit. A couple of. 50 caliber machine guns are exposed, the coverings are removed as the armed men and women, while backing away, apply a few blows with their rifles to those on the outside of the group of civilians, ensuring no one decides to remove themselves from the herd. The tension mounts. I look at Gunny. He's on the radio. He got through. I listen for good news! None comes.

A voice of command perpetrates the noisy villagers, and they go silent. "CALLATE!" It becomes instantly silent, even the jungle creatures stopping their incessant chatter, listening. In the silence, I hear the metal-on-metal slide noise of the weapons' bolts being pulled back and released.

Gunny hands me the handset, a blank look on his face. I search his eyes, trying to get a glimpse of what's going on inside his head. He looks up, to get everyone's attention. He twirls his index finger in the air, in a circular motion. Time to saddle up. What? Apparently, big brother has the info he needs, I think to myself. I look at the other Marines, trying to see some reaction, some type of human emotion; is this really what I signed up for, a massacre about to happen, and we do nothing? I don't care if there are 20 of them, and just a few of us... What the fuck?

I didn't become a Marine to witness something like this, I joined up to do something about shit like this. Fuck you, and fuck you, and fuck this shit! There's no fucking way I'm going to leave.

I think about all this to myself, for what seems like an eternity, and look up as I feel fingers coming towards my neck. Sgt. Crabtree grips the lymph nodes right near my ears with his fingers, to get my attention. How did he know, do we all go through this, how could... could they possibly have seen this before? Is this really what it's like, this job? He looks at me, close and intense, he looks right into my eyes, with the utmost, deepest compassion a warrior can muster towards another, who is realizing for the first time, what this life shit is all about. Your eyes get opened forever... Once you see the inherent disregard for human life, you change.

Just then, the two .50 caliber, full automatic machine guns, plus the various other rifles, erupt below. Screaming ensues. Women, children, and men are being cheesed with a multitude of rounds, zipping through them faster than the speed of sound. The lucky ones never hear a retort from any rifle, just maybe the burning feeling of that incorrigible lead, urging itself through their body.

I hear not one, but, three babies crying, one has an all out wail going. You know the kind, the kind that pierces your eardrums, causing angst, and you don't know who's going to do it, but, somebody has to fix it, now, give the baby what it wants, figure it out and make it stop kind of sound. I cannot believe I hear that, over all the concussions going on down there. The smells of gunpowder, copper, and shit, rise to burn our nostrils.

The voiced commands from below enter my ears, as the gunfire comes to a halt. "Revisalos!" a bored voice says.

Bang. one pistol shot, a baby stops crying. ***Bang.*** A

85

second pistol shot. One screaming banshee continues, but, that next shot just never comes. The screaming and the wailing from the baby continues... no shot! Where's the third shot? Shoot the fucking baby.

I cannot believe I just thought that!

We're doing our final check, making sure to leave nothing behind, while they make sure, down in the clearing, that they leave no live ones behind. Random single gun shots ring out, murmurs, crying, and pleas fade away. Being as quiet as possible, knowing it has been ten minutes, and the patrol should be by any minute now, unless they stopped to watch, as well. Maybe they saw it and ran, appalled at the senselessness of it all. Running down there right now, to shoot the man in charge, to help save that fucking baby that's still crying.

It's time to go. We start out, heading North slightly, to create some space between us and the patrols. We pause, just before the next patrol arrives. We will let it go by. When I hear them coming it's obvious, they hadn't run down the hill to save the day, and the people. Instead, they are chatting and flirting with each other, just like they had been the last time around. Nonchalant as all get out, not giving a shit about... ***Bang.***

Finally, the banshee scream of the last baby has stopped. Fuck me. I just rooted for it. I'm thankful for it, even.

15

Anger rages inside me. I want to kill them, all of them, every fucking person that had participated in killing all those unarmed people. How can they just shoot humans like that? Fuck. This is really happening. Mock future conversations go through my head:

"What did you do in the Marines, man?

Nothing really, nope, I didn't do anything. I mean, I watched a bunch of women and children get killed, right alongside their parents and grandparents. But, I didn't do anything about it, just watched, and then caught my helicopter ride home, in order to get back for the weekend.

No, I didn't stop it. Why? 'Cause I wasn't allowed to intervene. Where you ask? Well, you'll never know, it didn't make the news. Genocide rarely makes the news."

Man, what I would do for an AT-4 right now. In the moment, I wish we carried heavy, I'd love to blow all those motherfuckers up. The rage in me is to be bottled, and harnessed, and caged.

Probably forever.

As I get up on my haunches, to ready myself for the long haul over the ridge-line, I steal a look down below, instantly wishing I had not, but, how could I not.

The rains have started. An invisible drizzle soaks everything, big drops find their way off the giant leaves, the accumulation of the mist being the culprit. Without warning, the rains increase to a downpour. Through this filter, I imprint the sights below onto the back of my retinas, forever to be seen.

The people are roughly splayed about in a group along one edge of the clearing, steam emitting from the pile. From here, I see torn clothing, blood, and the looks of lasting horror, engraved on faces. Seeing the men, women, and kids all in the same pile, suffering the same fate, has me wondering what they did to deserve this. My brain has a thought to look for the three babies, but, luckily, I dismiss it. Somehow my eyes pick out the little old lady, with her multi-colored outfit, splattered with a new, deep red-colored paint, her arm is outstretched and splayed across the woman beside her. This woman, the one with the baby swaddled in her shawl, lay dead, eyes open, staring at the sky, half of her baby's head is gone, the blood and brains splattered across her chest. Suddenly, I know the woman on patrol would not hesitate to kill me.

16

We make our way to the LZ. The landing zone is only a click and a half away from our current position, on the other side of a ridge. We move quickly, and in silence. Not because of what just happened, because this is how we move. Swift, silent... and deadly, as needed.

No signs of worry cross the painted faces of the Marines I am with. I'm sure my war face is back in place, as well. I shut the lid to that tight little box of memories, the moment we were on the move. No time for that right now. This isn't the time for the distractions. This story must be told, and if we die, it won't be. Hyper focus is my being, I am invisible, I am silent. I move as a ghost, no scent, see-thru mode, no tracks left behind. All my senses are alive! My body is tingling, the electricity in it, setting the body on fire. Every bird, bug and movement, is now recorded subconsciously, in my brain. A brain map is put together, and adapted, as I move through the jungle. The tree and animals are added before me, as others roll off the mental map, far enough behind, to no longer be needed. Unless we turn around. Then the map will magically re-appear. The wind brings nothing, but, rotting organic matter, and the smells of the wild animals' fear, at the presence of humans, to my nostrils.

The hair on my neck alert and ready, is still at rest. When we crest the ridge, near our LZ, that changes. Unaware of this, barn-sour and ready for a cheeseburger, I don't pay attention to their silent alert, instead focusing on the rumble in my stomach. I guess that's a good sign.

The signal to freeze, then get down, is passed through the group. We oblige. After a moment, we all gather up and look down at the LZ. It is a perfect spot, a flat clearing in this jungle, strongly held by a huge group of people, dressed in uniforms and armed the same as the group we encountered earlier. As we watch, the big trucks and other vehicles can also be heard   approaching. This landing zone is dead, we'll have to make haste to LZ-2.

17

We're slinking off, heading in a new direction, either to misdirect any possible pursuers, or heading to a new LZ. If I had eavesdropped while Gunny was on the horn, I would know. Instead, I was, per usual, distracted by what's going on in my head. Suddenly, we all freeze, not conscious as to why, until I hear running. Someone, no, several some ones, are running toward us. I stay frozen, since no order to move has come. The timing could not be worse for Sgt. Crabtree and I, we're in a clearing in the jungle. Then the command comes, "70 yards left. Go!"

Sgt. Crabtree and I move fast. Sticking together, we move 90 degrees to the left of the direction we were just moving. We cover about a third of that 70 yards, when we come to a small cliff side.

Looking up, we know we have to go around, only 12 feet from where we're standing to the top, would be do-able, if we helped each other, yet, this mini-cliff is small enough to go around and then proceed onward. We go around.

That little delay is enough for some pursuers behind us to get a line of sight on us. A shot rings out, a chill goes up my spine, as I hear a *pfffft* sound go by my ear, and I feel the movement of air. A bullet just missed me! Damn!

I find a way to move faster.

Now around the cliff face, we run up the small hill, once cresting the top, we start moving faster, suddenly Sgt. Crabtree stops and moves behind some cover. He withdraws his K-bar, and waits.

I guess he's done with this running shit.

After a millisecond's hesitation, more like a pause in motion, I keep moving. Maybe the pursuers will run right by him. I dive over the long root of a tree, shaped like some ancient buttress, it's long and skinny. Once I hit soft soil on the other side, I turn myself around and poke my head and rifle over it. Just in time to see a mustachioed pursuer run even with the tree Sgt. Crabtree is hiding behind. And as he does, Sgt. Crabtree comes out with knife at the ready. From my perspective, it seems he holds the knife out in front of the man and lets him run through it. The sharp knife, made for such an event, slices through the soft skin of the throat area and back to the spine, the spine pushes it out of the way as the man stops running, and stumbles. He somehow stays on his feet and grabs for his throat, accidentally pushing his head backwards, off of it. It hinges there, as the body falls to the ground.

In the distance, I hear gunshots, apparently, there are other pursuers out here. I walk towards the body, as does Sgt. Crabtree, it's one of the two we saw patrolling, earlier. We both listen for movement besides our minimal noise. We hear nothing nearby. Others can be heard yelling to each other, and pursuing the rest of the team, but, they seem to be beyond us now. We'll have some catching up to do.

Before we can, we hear a woman demand us to "ALTO!" stop, she says. We freeze. Or I do at least, I look up and she's about five feet from me. We didn't even hear, or feel her! Sgt. Crabtree is a little closer to her. He turns towards the armed woman, K-bar knife at the ready, I also turn towards her, she pulls the trigger of the rifle in her hands. The bullet goes into Sgt. Crabtree's left leg, taking him down hard, onto the dirt. "Ugh!" is the only sound that escapes his lips. I see the pain come to the surface, yelling to come out, he jams his right hand into his mouth and clamps down on it.

I turn and lunge for the woman's midsection, applying a deep shoulder into her solar plexus, I knock the wind out of her, while driving her up off her feet. In the same motion, I pull behind the knees and lift slightly to drive the woman onto the flat of her back. What minuscule air she had loitering in the bottoms of her lungs is expelled on impact, as is the rifle from her hands. Not being able to think beyond not being able to breathe, she lay there shocked, only for a second, then realizes I'm making a move to be on top of her. Too late, she springs into action, attempting to roll aside, wanting me to miss. I now gain the power position anyway, shooting through before she can turn, my left leg catching the inside of hers, just in time to prevent her from moving.

Coming to a landing in the power position, I attempt a rifle butt-stroke to her face.

The position and the length of the M-16A2 rifle make it an awkward attempt from this close proximity. She rolls her head to the side, easily avoiding the swinging end of the rifle. This miss, combined with my pack weight's desire to meet up with the gravity of the earth, pulls me half off of her.

Having lost my power position, I now look at the top of her head, being the only thing within striking distance. I smack at it with the side of my rifle butt. The dull sound of a spring encased in heavy duty plastic, hitting the top of her skull, creates a stick and basketball-type sound, three quick whacks at her head. I scramble off her and gain my knees. She sits up and briefly gives me the back of her head, I swing a good strong butt-stroke at the sweet spot on the back of the neck, knowing it will end her. But, she moves! Spinning her body around she faces me, knees planted on the damp earth, toes at the ready (*at least on my part*), I still have my rifle in my hands, she has nothing in hers. Yet, still, one of us is about to die.

Pointing the business end of my rifle at her for the first time, I consider going loud. Sure, she's already fired a shot, but, one is hard to locate, especially in this type of terrain. A second one, while everybody is listening for it, is an entirely different story. Aiming the M-16 directly at her, she rests on her knees panting, grateful to have air in her lungs again; knowing that if she moves, I will pull the trigger. I have to decide, now.

Still pointing my weapon at her, I slowly stand up. I will have to make the third time the charm. One good butt-stroke to the temple is cleaner, more efficient, and safer than pulling the trigger.

Maybe she sees the look in my eye, or just decides to act out of desperation, who knows, I will never know until the afterlife, if there is one. Regardless, she grabs a handful of dirt and attempts to throw it at me. At this time, Sgt. Crabtree's hand and K-bar knife appear over the woman's left shoulder, and I watch the knife, as it is driven straight down through the bone gap into her body cavity. The look on the woman's face instantly changes to shock. Eyebrows go up into the hairline, the jaw gapes open, and spittle escapes into the air, fleeing the scene. Eyes. The eyes bulge to the point of no return, turning red in the instant. I see the knife wielding hand move in a tight circle and then it quickly withdraws. The knife, sends a short-lived squirt of blood outwards, as the lifeless woman sinks down to the earth, smacking her face finitely into it. Gravity wins. Sgt. Crabtree and I make eye contact, yep, we are both OK.

"You search her, I'll dress my gunshot. It's a "through and through", missed bone, I'll be fine. Maybe not to walk, but, whew..." he says, the last part to no one in particular.

Without hesitation, I approach the dead woman and pull up her pant legs to see if she has anything hidden there, or down in her boots, work my way up her body, turning out pockets as I go: cigarettes, zippo, a tamale wrapped in its' traditional corn masa, and then, a more modern wrap of wax paper. I pile everything up on her belly as I check her neck area and head cover for any other items, finding no pictures or items containing writing at all, to say anything of military or identifying characteristics. I then consider keeping the tamale for later, but, deciding against it, I place her items back into her pockets.

Finished with my task, I help Sgt. Crabtree with his wound treatment. Like he said, it's a through and through; having hit nothing to mushroom it, other than military muscle, the 7.62mm still left a decent exit wound. The area is quickly swelling and turning an angry purple and dark blue. Tightly, we apply the bandages, one on the entry side and one on the exit. Pulling the cotton straps, we wrap them and tie a knot over each wound. Pulling the remnants of his pant leg back into place, I wrap an olive drab sling dressing around the outside, to help keep them, and the material he had cut to get to the wound, in place.

That done, I look at him, "OK, what next?" feeling super stretched already, my internal rookie is feeling the effect of the day thus far.

"OK, I'm good to go here, you'll have to carry me, or leave me to get help. First, let's hide that body!" he says.

We move the dead woman up to the buttress roots of the tall, straight-trunked tree. Branchless to its' top, where a great canopy escapes in all directions, the tree claims space with it and the giant legs spreading in multiple directions, away from its' center. Tall root systems create rooms made of three sides, up against its' trunk. We pull the woman to that buttress area of the tree. Moving the earth quickly with my feet, and Sgt. Crabtree with the K-bar back in his hands, we pull aside the deep pilings of leaves and rotting matter. Pulling enough aside to create a cavity, I pull and roll the dead woman into it, only partly underground. We push all the organic matter back on top of her and camouflage the body with it. Surely, humans will not find her body until after the scavengers do, but, by then, it will be too late.

Feeling a little safer up against the tree's base, I take a moment to stand up straight and stretch my back. The radio's weight and the other items in my backpack felt heavy in that instant. I arch my shoulders backward and work my neck for a while, looking around. Everything seems fine, I think to myself. Amazing barometric-type change I already have, to the definition of what is fine.

While I'm stretching, Sgt. Crabtree slings his rifle and puts his K-bar back into its' sheath. Without talking, we already know what we're going to do. Since he's awake and OK, he stands himself up, using the buttress as a backrest, he pushes up against it with his good leg and his arms. Before I can protest, he's standing up, leaning against the tree for support. Not one to leave him hanging, I move in and scoop him up. Swinging my right arm through his crotch area and up his spine, the left arm helping to guide his right arm around my neck, I arch my back and stand tall. I bounce Sgt. Crabtree slightly to get him in a good position on my shoulders, trying to balance him, while he adjusts to the discomfort of having my radio sticking into him. My arm over his right leg, I grab his left wrist to help hold him in place and gently reach down and grab my M-16 by the handle.

Gunny will be wondering where we are by now, I think to myself. I want to get there quick. It would suck for them to have to cover the same ground twice. They'll either be waiting, or heading back this way to check on us. Gaining that trained-in focus, I start covering the ground I need to cover.

Gy/Sgt Pazorski is, indeed, waiting for us. I'm glad they were not worried enough to retrace their steps. They were instead, in hasty defensive positions, facing outboard in all general directions, Gunny himself looking back from whence they had come; attention and much concern all over his face, when he comes into my view.

We must've been a sight to see. My 135-pound frame carrying Sgt. Crabtree's stocky frame on my shoulders. Thankfully, he's short and stocky, not tall and stocky.

Regardless, Gunny's first sights of me, has me focused, breathing like crazy, sweating like a pig on a spit, I'm red-faced and flush, I would have had to take a break here soon and I'm grateful to see Gunny's ugly mug looking back at me.

Not one to give up, I carry Sgt. Crabtree to their position, and deposit him as gently as possible in our current conditions, to the ground. He thuds a bit and rolls onto his back. Leaning over, I pant and catch my breath, Cpl. Alvarez motions for me to crouch down, and I take a position next to Sgt. Crabtree. Gunny comes up and gets the skinny from Sgt. Crabtree on what happened.

I have time to think (*not a good thing*). I should've shot her. Fuck. Sgt. Crabtree is laying on the ground bleeding from a gunshot wound, and he had to finish her off. But, then again, I would do that too, I suppose; Hell, if she was presented before me like that, I would help a brother out. It's not like this is a fight in the octagon, with rules, is it? And it's not like this is about a fair fight. Did those villagers get a fair deal? Not even close. Amazing to me, what people will do to each other. I thought I had a pretty good idea before joining up, but, I had no idea, really.

I joined the Marines for a wake-up call. I got one, didn't I? I wasn't prepared for what humans do to each other, on purpose. It's almost as if there's a sickness that overtakes us from time to time, and we go all bat shit crazy, and start killing each other for no apparent reason, other than some HMFIC decides to, and we all go, "OK. Duh, sure, why not. Let's kill them all, then we can do it your way, without anybody speaking an opinion on the matter." At least, the Germans are apologetic on the subject. All the other nations choose to play dumb about the genocide and slavery in their history. They're all like, "What? We didn't do anything." They call that denial, by the way, people.

Is there an empire in history created without slavery, or slave-like labor? Name one, then go look it up, I'm sure you'll find it in there. All the way back to the Egyptians and before, Romans after that, British empire, America for sure. Maybe the only one not, would be Russia, hell, when the weather is like that!?! But, then again, maybe I just don't know their history enough, there's definitely tyranny involved, and genocide. Is genocide part of the natural way of things, as well? Is there an area of the world that has not participated in that?

I feel a hand on my shoulder, "You good-to-go Marine?" It's Gy/Sgt Pazorski checking on me. I had left the building again. Looking up and making eye contact, I say, "I'm set, Gunny. Just thinking again." I smile at him so he knows I'm not freaking out on him, just day-dreaming, as usual. "I'm wondering if there's a natural order to genocide and slavery. It seems to be a requirement for some reason, in human history," I whisper to him.

"Well, good luck with that kid. In the meantime, good job back there, Sgt. Crabtree says you did good."

"I could've done better," I reply.

"Of course, and we could've been there with you guys. But, I made that decision," he looks at me. Suddenly, I get an inkling of what leadership is about.

"Yes, sir," I say.

He gives me a look for calling him sir. Which I usually do when he has said something simple, yet profound, and taught me something without trying. He hates it. I love it.

"I don't know if you guys heard it, but, we missed our ride, we have to head for the next LZ. They can't risk flying into this area again. Take five more and then we'll head out. Call 'em and let 'em know we're headed for LZ number 3. Third times a charm!" he whispers while smiling, and then goes about his business.

I get them on the horn and communicate that we know we missed, no details conveyed over the horn, except to let them know we have a walking wounded. Although technically, he won't be doing much walking, or maybe he will, depends on what type of pain drugs that we're carrying, I guess. Speaking of, reaching into my chest pocket, I grab a few grunt candies. Grunt candy is known to most as Ibuprofen, nothing like a few of these to make the pains go away.

18

We've been running for our third, and hopefully final, pickup for a duration of about four hours, it seems like just minutes, and days, at the same damn time. It really is amazing how painfully fast torture can be, sometimes it's almost as if it's needed. Needed to toughen the mind and soul.

Needed to feel it all, and put it into perspective. Everything is easy, compared to that day, in that unnamed place, where that thing we saw didn't really happen, but, someone needed to know if it were happening, if it was. And they better do something, I better be hearing about this through scuttlebutt, pretty soon. America sends aid to the rebels, or, is it the rebels doing the deed, and we have to send aid to the other side? I don't even know which side that was down there. I have a pretty good idea, but, no way of knowing for sure. I'm just a Lance Corporal, I can't believe I have to make these decisions... Wait. WTF? I don't, I'm a Lance. I just do my job.

I look up at Gy/Sgt. Pazorski. I'm ready, it is seen, and we are on the move again. One more time, we pause to rest and listen, hard to hear at such a fast pace. Our usual quiet-at-all-cost mentality, is lifted enough for us to move at a faster rate. We're still quieter than high school kids sneaking out a bedroom window, but, not like our usual quieter than a ghost level.

Given a moment to snack and regroup my senses, I go back to my head: WTF. So much for an easy first mission. Throw him to the wolves, more like. Anyone who shoots that many people, doesn't want it to be found out, and anybody who has the power to capture 200 people, isn't going to let it slide, either. Dare I say, I'm having fun, in a way? What the fuck, we're just tear-assing through the woods, on a mission from Hell to home, in order to live. Talk about an incentive program.

You can be anything you want to be, the recruiter says… interesting. How do I say, all the adventure without the death of buddies, and only killing people I'm 100% sure are bad guys? Just like the cartoon heros, right? He-Man always knew who the bad guy was, and none of his buddies ever died. Or, is that just how I remembered it? I wonder just how I'll remember this mission? It was a walk in the park, cool stroll in the jungle, no worries mate, it's just a walk-up, non-technical.

Too late, I hear a footstep… at first, I thought I was the first one to hear it, then I noticed Gunny was more invisible than usual. I swallowed my breath, this fucker was close. Too late to unsnap my K-bar, my rifle butt was going to have to do. Goodbye cherry. Someone is headed directly toward me, and my position is not good. My boonie hat is above the ground cover, my eyes floating below my boonie's lid. Did I remember to paint my eyelids, or should I keep them open, I ask myself. I'm wanting to look more at the ground, than anything else, at this point.

He's quiet as a cat. A cat that's about to pounce, he knows we're nearby. He can sense it, or smell it, or just has plain ol' good instinct. He comes to me slouched and looking, SKS rifle in his hands, deftly, ready, practiced. He breezes by gunny. I tense my muscles, ready to spring, willing myself to pay attention to my recent training, not my recruit training, and not yelling out "kill" at the top of my lungs. Swift, silent, and deadly, is my motto now. Invisible and gone.

Teeth appear behind him, smiling, then Gunny catches himself, and the teeth disappear back to green. Gunny floats out behind the man sneaking up on us, seeking us. I see the look of realization cross his face, as a hand goes over his chin and grabs it in a quick death grip. Another arm reaches around with a nimbly gripped K-bar: quick, effortless, the sharp knife cuts to the spine. Not a sound, or seeming motion is made, yet, it was done. Later, I would swear I heard a breath escaping the throat, yet, would rather believe it was the wind. Gy/Sgt Pazorski, slowly, as quietly as possible, pulls the lifeless body into the shadows. I check the ground, nary a drag mark, but, I cleanse the area anyway. I can't believe we've still managed to stay quiet. Although, at a rate of five miles in two hours, our chances of getting away are dwindling. Hey, not bad for a few guys fleeing the worst thing this one's ever seen, and still can't be easy for Sgt. Crabtree. I mean a through and through, is still a gun shot.

I see Sgt. Crabtree is holding his shit together successfully. I hope my surface looks the same. Gunny and Sgt. Cowan seem to not have skipped a beat at all. So, in fact, it is possible to move on from this, maybe get used to it even. I look forward to that day, nary an emotion. Being numb might be a good thing, after all.

19

We rest, hidden, partway down a cliff side, formed by the slow erosion of the limestone dolomite. The culprit, is an ancient rain-fed river, now located about 30 yards below us. Pointman had scoped out a drainage and found this perch conveniently located out of sight, but, within hearing distance of a well-traveled local trail, that runs along the natural and relatively vegetation free zone, near the cliff's edge.

The trail wanders the perimeter between the riparian zone and the high altitude jungle. Strikingly colorful birds fly back and forth between the protection of the canopy and the water below. Long, iridescent tails flow behind them as they zip up and down. Their tails appear to be green, or gold, hard to tell. Either the sun changes them, or this is part of their natural design. One lands nearby and tilts his head in our general direction. Shit! I watch him with trepidation, if he squalls an alarm, we'll be on the move in half a heartbeat.

So far, we've been lucky, no monkeys have howled, no birds have screamed at us, and Sgt. Crabtree's biggest fear, has not come to fruition: being eaten by a giant cat. We all have our things, and Sgt. Crabtree's phobia is being eaten by a giant cat. I couldn't help but laugh when, over beers, he told me this. How poetic is it, that our first long range mission, is to an area that is full of Cougars and Jaguars, which is why he watches the trees, relentlessly. Sgt. Crabtree has a great chance of stepping into a trap, or on a snake, since his eyeballs are obsessed with the trees.

Being the good friend that I am, I compensate by keeping my eyes on the ground, and scoping all those hazards, since he has the tree sniper and wild cat thing under control.

The fancy bird decides that we're no threat and he begins preening himself while he is perched overhead. I watch him do his thing, and I'm amazed at the vibrancy of his feathers. They shimmer and change from green to gold, as he moves each feather from its' home, to remove all dust and dirt, returning it properly when he's finished. Very shortly, a mass of these birds join him and they hang out with us while we take a break. Gunny is on duty while we all rest and shut down. Having already taken my Marine nap, I enjoy this chance to "legally" daydream, and check out the local ecosystem.

For those not familiar with the term, I'm sure we all have a name for it: Cat nap, power nap, post lunch nap. My Grandpa is famous for taking couch naps on the weekend and holiday afternoons, it didn't matter what's going on in the world, or how many of us are in the house, he just assumes the position, usually in his outdoor/shop clothes, dirty and ripped up, they hang on him and make him look like a semi-hobo. "Why wear good clothes to get dirty in, the misses will just give me hell! So, I wear clothes that would make her drop dead, if

106

she saw me headed to town in."

Yes, the same clothes grace the couch each afternoon, while he checks out for 10-20 minutes. Sometimes (*like holidays*), the house is in complete chaos, the talking and footsteps are all echoing around the ground floor of the house, but, within minutes of grandpa assuming the nap position, the news travels through the house in a whisper, and all goes quiet for the duration of his nap, and usually, even longer, as his actions are contagious and many take their opportunity for a break from the family, by either napping in their own respective corners, or heading outside to wander the back forty acres. Others head to the store, or sip tea on the porch. I'm amazed at this silent version of setting another example.

The sun uses the river created gap in the canopy to shine its' brilliance on my face. Feeling what is left of my grease paint soften in the sun, I take some earth and rub it about my face, blending it with the camo paint I put there, a day or so ago. I do have some paint with me, but, dirt is quicker and easier at this point. The sweat and grease will help hold it in place, and it has less shine than sweaty camo paint. Sitting there, leaning against the stone wall, knees bent with feet flat on the ground, I rest against my pack and radio, my rifle slung over and under behind me, it rests on my pack as well. I hold the .45 caliber 1911 in my hand, safety on, a better weapon for this locale.

Turning my face into the sun, I close my eyes again, feeling the sun and looking at the glow through my eyelids. I contemplate nothing, and just listen to it all. The birds doing their thing, talk softly amongst themselves while they preen. The river flowing down below, ripples and gurgles its' delight at its' uninhibited path.

The light breathing of the men next to me, as it blends with the winds moving down the river canyon, are the sounds that enter my ears. Eyes closed, I realize I am napping again, when I'm startled awake by the sudden sound and feeling of a rush of air and all the long-tailed birds take flight at once, squawking in protest, feathers ruffle and beat off each other, they flee the scene for parts unknown.

Something's coming. Chances are, it's a bunch of pigs, or Sgt. Crabtree's jaguar. Listening, I hear quick moving steps, vivacious, they move with authority. They are not steps of pigs or cats. Rather the booted feet of humans.

Looking about, I see the others are awake. I push myself into the cliff and very softly, disengage the safety of my 1911 pistol. Looking up and behind me, I see I'm in a well-hidden position. The cliff overhang above me, keeps my legs and boots invisible to prying eyes from above. Cpl. Alvarez is located closest to the drainage coming down from above and will have first dibs on all who come within reaching distance.

Several pairs of feet go stomping by, covering ground they move with reckless abandon, obviously in a hurry to do something. Suddenly a set of boots stops their forward progress and comes to the limestone edge above us. They stand there for just a couple moments, before the owner's voice is heard. He calls to someone in Spanish. I hear another set of boots stroll on over. The two converse for several minutes before moving on. They move quickly, but, not in a hurry just the same.

My curiosity is aroused, there are only two of us that speak Spanish, and I'm not one of them: Sgt. Crabtree and Gunny Pazorski are the two. Funny enough, Cpl.

Alvarez does not, having grown up in an orphanage. I watch my friend out of the corner of my eye. From where I'm perched, he looks a little bit worried and confused. We all sit quiet and wait for Gunny to come down from where he's hidden, just above. I'm sure he pulled a chameleon when the two men approached our resting spot. We all hear the quiet boot steps coming down the drainage and wait in anticipation, hoping it's Gunny, which it is. He comes over to the middle of us quietly, and motions for us to wait and be silent. We all continue to listen and feel for a couple of minutes, in case of stragglers, or returning soldiers. After few minutes, Sgt. Crabtree and Gunny start talking, quietly.

Ending their intense conversation with both nodding in agreement, Sgt. Crabtree duck walks over to me, keeping his profile low and his motions quiet. Whispering he says, "We need you to get on the horn."

I look around. It's about as open as it gets, and the river helps. Not so much with deflecting of the radio waves, but, in giving them a clear path to the sky. It's up to the ethers after that.

"I can put an antenna up in the tree. That will help." I point to the tree that was filled with luminous birds not long ago. "If it's important, that'll increase our chances. What are the chances someone else will come along?" I'm wondering about the animal and human used pathway. I'll be exposed to it, and the other side of the river bank to some degree, as well.

"Do it." he says.

"OK. If I fall, catch me will ya?" I say smiling.

"What? Are you kidding me, you're part billy goat, you can climb anything." He pats me on the shoulder making a slight noise. We both wince, instinctively. I pull a long, rolled up antenna from my pack, carried for this very purpose. Who knew climbing cliffs and trees was a radioman's job requirement. Heck, being good at everything, is beneficial in this job.

Cpl. Alvarez offers to help me out by changing out the battery, while I climb and unfurl the antenna, as high up in the tree as it allows. Tree climbing is one of those things almost every boy loves, and some, like me, never outgrow it. Gaining about 30 feet of the tree in no time, I find a way to, at least temporarily, attach the antenna to a tree limb using zip ties. And wind it a couple of times around the main trunk on my way down, getting back to the radio as Cpl. Alvarez has finished the changeover. I get BIG1 on the radio and hand it over to Gunny.

"BIG1 this is Waldo, come in, over," he whispers into the handset and repeats.

"This is BIG1, go ahead Waldo, good to hear from you, over," the voice on the radio says.

"We're hard charging and good to go, for Honeypot 3, sir. One walking wounded, and all others sound and clean, over," Gunny says.

"Outstanding Waldo, Bumble Bee is on schedule for 14 hundred. Have pots gathered and ready for pickup, over," the voice says.

Grinning, Gunny replies, "Looking forward to it, over." His face changes to that of one giving bad news to someone. "BIG1, BIG1, this is Waldo. One more thing, over."

"Go ahead Waldo, over."

Talking quietly into the radio Gy/Sgt Pazorski informs them that our previous intel was incomplete, and that based on a conversation he and Sgt. Crabtree can confirm, the units we saw, are actually, government troops, dressed as Rebels. They're disguising themselves, in order to....

Wait! What? Did I hear him right? I look over to Sgt. Crabtree and he just nods slightly, fluttering his eyes in disgust.

So, the head motherfuckers in charge, are killing off their own people, in order to what? I purposely know nothing about world politics. But what, drugs? Control? What could justify killing off the people they're supposed to take care of....... yeah, yeah, I know. Not mine to reason why.

Finishing his conversation, Gunny hands me the handset, which I place back on the radio and police up a few things of mine, I cinch up the inner liner and clip the pack-flap, and as I have a thousand times before, I put the Alice pack in its' place on my back. Somehow it seems heavier than it did when I took it off, just a short while ago. Perhaps Cpl. Alvarez put some rocks or the extra battery he was carrying in it. He's a non-hacker if he did. Doesn't matter, I can hump it out, I can hack it. Even if, in all reality, it's a little more weight of the world in there, I can hack it. No seabag drag here.

I arch my back slightly while still on my knees, pulling down my blouse top, tucking my t-shirt into my trousers, before clasping the giant plastic buckle at my waist. As I'm leaning forward, I rub some of the tree's dirt out of the dead muskrat that lives on my head, and replace my boonie cover back in its' place. Working my hands around the brim, I place it just above the ears. After adjusting the string so that the back sides are up and off my ears a bit, to free up my peripheral vision and improve hearing ability, I pull down the front brim a bit to cover my eyes (*the whites are a dead giveaway*). I'm really hoping to run into these guys again. I re-sling my rifle and pull out my pistol and K-bar, one in each hand.

Gunny looks at me, "What are you doing? We aren't going after them... We're getting out of here," he says. Looking down at my hands, I realize what I had been getting ready for and shrug my shoulders, to no one in particular. He just smiles, pats me on the shoulder, and moves out and up the drainage.

When leaving: "Which way do we go, Gunny? Up or down. We could move really fast down there, it's pretty free of underbrush, mostly rock," Cpl. Alvarez says.

"It's a death zone down there. If they double back and see us, we're fubar," says Sgt. Crabtree.

"What he said," Gy/Sgt Pazorski replies, "We'll go up high and follow them, we just happen to be headed in the same direction, except no trail for us, we're going a level or two higher on the rock, to traverse as quickly as we can to our third LZ option, just on the other side of this ridge. It's closing time boys, it's 2 am, and the only option is the drunk lady semi-passed out in the corner, that you need serious beer goggles for. And we're gonna take her like we've been waiting our entire lives for her."

"If we don't, we're walking home, aren't we, Gunny?" I ask.

"Exactly, Big1 won't risk another, not with Sgt. Crabtree able to walk."

We look at him as he smiles at us, in his drug high, "It's gonna hurt like a mutha come tomorrow, but, I'm good to go, to walk all the way home. How far is it as the crow flies?" he asks.

"About 1,500 miles, I'm guessing," I say.
"Ooof," he says, "Let's catch this chopper!"

20

We stand just over the other side of the ridge, our LZ in sight. Except it isn't a "landing zone" after all. It's a small clearing down below us, formed by a rock outcropping, not big enough for a helicopter to land on, not even for these pilots. This will be an extraction.

"Take turns tying your hasty's," Gunny says. Cpl. Alvarez and I are now crouched next to each other, so we take turns watching our six and tying our swiss seats. I take out a rope we basically carry around for this purpose. Of course, I would use it for everything and anything, as needed. Today, I just need to remember how to tie a swiss seat. Or better yet, not think about it, and just do it. I look off, down the small valley, while my hands do their work. It's a great spot for a helicopter to veer off the main valley and swing in for a pickup. No fuss — no muss.

My harness tied, I crouch down and take watch as Cpl. Alvarez ties his. Taking out my knife and pistol, I feel like an idiot, and return them to their respective holsters. A rifle is way more appropriate for this situation. When Cpl. Alvarez is ready, he resumes watch, as I warm up the radio and get our final confirmation of our extraction.

"BIG1, BIG1 this is Waldo, over," I say.

They are on instantly, *"Waldo this is BIG1 one, proceed over,"* the voice on the other end says.

"Honeypots are full and ready for pickup, over," I speak into the handset.

"Bumble Bee is on schedule for liftoff Waldo, over," it says back to me.

"Outstanding BIG1. Over and out," I say and secure the radio's handset.

Every one of us is exhausted and ready to go. Our gear is secured in our packs and on our bodies. Our boonie covers are either in a leg pocket or tight on our heads. The helicopter comes at us, low and slow, as the pilot approaches. When just above, the rope is lowered. With no verbal communication, all but two of us attach ourselves with carabiners to the dangling rope, which has several attachment points, properly distanced from each other. When most of us are secured to the rope, the last two Marines secure themselves. Gy/Sgt Pazorski pulls on the rope hard a couple of times and we're lifted off the security of the earth, without warning. The speed of the chopper creates a wind that whisks all the sweat from my body in an instant. I shiver as my body temperature drops rapidly. As I observe the view I'm given by my location under the helicopter and chosen attachment point, I attempt to spot the government troops below. None. Nothing. I look around to get details of the location from above, hoping to someday figure out where we are, and tell the world what happened. Young, yet wise enough, more so than a week ago, I'm sure none of this will make the news. I wonder if anything we do will make the news.

Not if we do our jobs right. We're in the category of

"need to know," and honestly, civilians don't **want** to know, to say nothing about the need to know. That's why they keep us around, so they can live in bliss. I may never be able to though.

After picking us up off the ridge, the helicopter heads down to the valley below. Once there, it beelines for a big clearing, where the experienced pilot gently deposits us back to earth, and then flies away to pull up the rope and give us time to get out of the clearing, so he can land. We hastily set a perimeter, facing outboard. As soon as we're ready, the helicopter comes back around.

With a sigh of relief, he lands flat on the ground, rotors still turning, of course (*we aren't out of there, yet*). I get up off my knee with a decent amount of effort. Not there yet, on your toes Marine, I tell myself. Head down, eyes squinting, I hoof it for the chopper, needing help running at the pace I want to, I take my hand and boonie off my head. The dirt glues to the sweat almost at the same instant the rotors try pulling it off my head. I relish the relief in temps again, as I climb on the chopper, claiming a spot on the deck, right about the middle. Gy/Sgt Pazorski sits in the seat behind me, facing forward to my left.

Cpl. Alvarez grabs the one next to him and Sgt. Crabtree climbs in, across from Gunny. The remaining team members fill the remaining spots. All are tired, and trying not to be too relieved, yet. After the last 24 hours, or so, who could blame us. Coincidently, the same pilot comes on the horn, *"If I'd known you guys liked me so much... how sweet, I woulda' come earlier, if I'da known..."*

I laugh in spite of myself. I think I've made it. I survived this motherfucker of a long-range mission. I wondered if they all will be like this, I just couldn't bear to ask. I figure if I'm ready for this every time, then I'll be up for it every time. Must be why we're such motherfuckers in training. Bleed in peace, only sweat in war, is that what they say? Gunny sat, staring off and down into the jungle, hard to read as always. He pulls a small hard case from his backpack. Pulling it apart he reveals several cigars. Grabbing one, he puts it in his mouth, and goes back to staring off into the below. He knows I'm watching him, "What Marine?" he says to me loud, to be heard over the wind and helicopter noise.

"I can't help but ask. How did you get used to it? Ho...."

"It's not my first rodeo Lance, you don't look at that shit, you just don't. There's no reason to, and lots of reasons not to."

It wasn't his first rodeo...

It was mine.

He hands me a cigar. I look at it and bringing it to my nose, I smell it deeply. I earned it. I'm still here after this day, more than an entire day ago, we got off of this exact helicopter. He looks down at me and says, "There is no way, any of this will ever be your fault."

30 years later, I heard him.

Putting the cigar up to my nose, I take another big whiff, it smells spicy and deep, earthy like the surface we just left. Putting it in a chest pocket, I lean my head back against the metal seat and webbing. Letting the ancient war-torn helicopter support me, as it vibrates all those thoughts out of my head.

21

We've been watching this compound long enough for me to know the ebb and flow of the periods between 4am-8am, noon-to-1600 hours, 2000-to-Midnight.

This time, our **"Observe and Report"** mission sends us to a high altitude jungle locale, in an unknown country. I'm sure Gy/Sgt Pazorski knows where we are, but, I'm still thriving on the plausible denial of not paying attention to where we are, and what's going on there. I stay sane and simple by focusing on the aspects of the mission, no need to reason why.

Dropped off at 0400, we settle in for an adjustment and listening period. Hunkering low into my long rest posture, a position that I can lay in for as long as needed, with just minor occasional adjustments to keep blood flowing. After checking to make sure my radio is off, and then one more time to be sure, I relax my body onto the earth. I feel minute particles swirling away and into my nostrils as I slowly breathe; dry and clingy, it leaves a film in the back of my throat and on the rear reaches of my tongue. Both dry out, turning them to jerky is the dust's goal.

Apparently even high altitude jungles, have a dry season. Resting my eyes for a moment, I open and close them a few times slowly, to bring on the night vision. While they're closed, my other senses roar to life. A light breeze works its' way into the underbrush, bringing with it the smells of the area. Scents of nighttime blooming flowers reach my senses; decaying organic matter, and the cool mountain air, intermingle in my nostrils.

After a moment, the smell of far off livestock becomes apparent. I even hear a few faint bleats of the sheep, surprised at first, that they would drop us so close to "civilization." I surmise the sounds and smells must be coming from down in the valley or, at least, the hillsides below.

The early morning air wafts them up to us. Surely, the same directional breezes sent the sounds of the chopper upwards into the vast atmosphere. At least, I like to think the "up tops", the Officers and Senior NCO's, have thought of this stuff…, Right?

No one on the team has moved since we established this position, a temporary one. I resist the urge to call it an L.P., although that is what we're currently doing, listening to determine what's going on around us, and letting our eyes adjust to the absolute darkness of a zero light situation. Although large units prefer to utilize the light of a fuller moon, to pull off their own endeavors, we prefer the light free situation of no, or little, moon. With only a few of us to keep track of, the darkness allows us more protection from peering eyes. One would have to be pretty damn close to us, to be able to detect the strange noise they thought they heard in the distance.

Accustomed to night maneuvers, and having met the

selection criteria of excellent night vision, we are stealthy, swift and silent in the night. Our gear is taped and attached so as to not make a sound, either from banging off each other, or from a face-plant on the ground. Nothing like the distant sound of plastic or metal, to let the world know where we are. I see a motion to my left, Sgt. Cowen is turning his head towards me, apparently, the man to his left grabbed his attention as well... it must be time to move. Sgt. Cowen replaced Sgt. Crabtree. Last time I checked in with Sgt. Crabtree, he told me he's running again, "jones-ing" to be mission, yet, the Doctors haven't cleared him. Sgt. Cowen is a black man from inner city Detroit. He looks like a bulldog when in his cami's, 5' 9" and sinewy, his no-nonsense demeanor reminds me of my Heavy from boot camp.

The only drill instructors that we had labels for, where the Heavy, the Stress Monster, and the Senior. The senior drill instructor wore a literally shiny, black belt. He was the strict father figure, really strict. When it was his turn to overnight in the DI hut, he would sit us in a circle and talk to us. Yes, talk to us. Can you believe it? All the while, chewing on cigar tobacco. Not the cigar. He would rip off pieces of it with his teeth, and keep it in his mouth. Spitting the offal into a container.

The Heavy — He was the one that found ways to get physical with you. Squeeze your fingers in a padlock, if you loosened them during drill, or standing at attention, anywhere. Tap shins with his boot tips, poke you with the brim of his cover, hit you with the pugil stick, after winning the pugil stick competition. Really, we were supposed to dodge it. Take it, and keep our focus, he was teaching me focus.

The Stress Monster, well the label says a lot. Ours was North Carolina Catawba tribe, Indigenous American. He stood 6' tall and had to be 200 pounds. He would get so riled up, he would turn a deep red, and pace back and forth, all the while making frantic hand motions and repeating the words, "Are you kidding me, you must be kidding me." Then stop, and stare at you, with huge eye balls, and sweat dripping off of him.

Sgt. Cowen moves slow, no noise is made. Reaching out with his right hand, he goes to touch my arm. Instead, I put my hand up and meet him. As soon as he feels my hand, he taps it twice. It is time to move. I retract my hand and pull my best slow motion snake move from my short-lived 8th grade break-dancing days, moving my body to the right, in order to pass on the message, Cpl. Alvarez already has the message and is moving in my direction, simultaneously.

We see each other and move back to our centers. Getting up slow, still observing and listening, I convince my body to move again, easy to do at this stage, with only 20 minutes of non-motion, the body did not have time to lock up.

All of us up and in our crouch, we wait a few moments longer and then we're on the move. To those not in the know, night travel is a farce, and a thing of the movies. Surely, only wildlife and people with night vision goggles, can move at night. We'll let them believe that. The rest of us know that with training, and some innate natural ability, night vision can be well developed.   We all may not be able to perform all-out sprints, like a lion hunting their prey, or the gazelle escaping said lion. But, yet again, with the same life or death incentive, we will. Running free through the darkness, dodging, weaving, all on instinct, is powerful. No time to over-think, the body knows what to do.

We've worked our way a few kilometers from our last position and now, we're on the opposite side of the ridge, down a few thousand feet in elevation. Below us, are a few barrels of flickering flames, and even a lantern light or two, escaping a window's coverings. This is the first village on our list. We're tasked with observing and reporting any notable activities.

Gy/Sgt Pazorski and Sgt. Cowen are going over the topographical map, while they are under a poncho; using the red lens cover on their moonbeam, keeps the glow of the light to a minimum.

The poncho hides the minimal noise of their musings, as well as, the red glow. The rest of the team faces outboard, listening and planting their eye's focus from spot to spot to spot, waiting for the peripheral vision to pick up any possible movement. I add to that routine, sometimes with my eyes totally closed, giving my ears, and sixth senses, a chance to pull in some sounds of living bodies, two-legged, or four. Either can be a precursor to discovery, giving away our position, and possibly forcing us to go live.

With my eyes closed, I note a small scurrying sound just outside my reach, a mouse of some sort is moving about, possibly gathering from his stores. I hear the breathing of the men around me, the slight rustle of the two men under the poncho, the faint and infrequent sounds of the village below, still quiet in the pre-dawn. A breeze creates the sound of a small stream about us, not enough to move the brush, but, enough to bring the scents and smells wafting up from below. That same, creosote-infected, metallic-tainted air, with the faint barnyard smell, intermingles with the smell of nothingness. The click of the moonbeam's off-switch signals the completion of the conference; slow and quiet, they remove themselves from their shelter, informing us that we're moving to a better position, before daylight comes.

Our proximity to the village below, has us moving more cautiously. Lots of time in the field, moving about at night, has given us the ability to, metaphorically, keep one eye on the horizon, and one eye on the dangers the earth holds. Stepping on a tripping hazard, hole in the ground, or small animal, can not only cause injury, but, the sounds of falling, wildlife interaction or pain escaping the lips, can lead to discovery. Discovery can lead to having to go loud, which is a penalty worse than death. Even the cliché' sound from all the movies and television shows, the ever present *'breaking stick'*, can lead to certain death for somebody.

So, we move with stealth, smooth and confident, our eyes and bodies scan everything around us. Calm, cool and collected, we exhaust our being, sensing what is not there, in case it is. Like ghosts, we move perpendicular gaining our new Observation Post, staying low to the ground, intermingled with the bush line, our silhouettes are nonexistent. Painted faces have no reflection and our taped down gear makes no noise. The occasional minuscule boot scrape, or a slow bend of some brush, the only giveaways to our presence.

Arriving at the chosen new location undetected, we settle in for the potential long haul. We each face outboard in our assigned locations around the base of a tree, surrounded by scrub brush, the tree canopy, and bushes, all combine to obscure us from all but the closest inquisitors. Yet, this will allow us a broad view around us, and the village below. We now are ***"discovery close"***. Close enough that some random villager or child, has the potential to come line of sight with us, during their daily wanderings.

As the sun comes up, I spot no trails or paths within my perspective view, which overlaps within eyesight of the Marine that I'm backed up on both sides by, our fields of vision overlapping. This way, when one of us is on a rest period, no movement is necessary to cover their field of responsibility. I can barely see the village on the right edge of my peripheral vision. To my left, the hills and mountainside gains elevation until it curves from view. I look parallel along the hillside, no trails to be seen.

Down below, the village is beginning its' morning wake-up routine. The roosters are crowing; how is it, everywhere in the world, there are roosters? A few children are playing quietly. The smoke and steam from morning cooking fires is multiplying. As I look, I notice this village is walled, I have to admit, I don't know exactly where we are, but, the inter-mountain transitional jungle gives an idea, we are fairly close to the equator.

Villages around here generally refrain from walling up their towns, the vast environment does a fairly good job of keeping unwanted things at bay, so they must really want to keep others out, or in. Perhaps that's why we're here, watching, to see who they're keeping in, or why they are keeping us out? Who knows at this point? To be honest, so far, I'm doing a kick ass job of not caring too much, why or what. Just that I'm here to observe and report. This being only my second mission, I'm content to learn from the more experienced Marines, and my brain is occupied with recalling training: where do I look? How's my distance? Not too close or too far from the Marine ahead of me, and ensuring the Marine behind me doesn't disappear? I still have this irrational fear of being grabbed when I'm Tail End Charlie. I watched too many old war movies, I guess, where the last guy on patrol has his throat slit, or is grabbed, only to be found later, tied to a tree with his own entrails. Well, maybe it isn't an irrational fear. Anyway, *"mine is not to reason why..."* formats in my mind, it helps me focus on things I have control over, like keeping the others in view, and not stepping on snakes, or tripwires.

A few hours later, with nothing notable happening, I feel movement behind me, knowing it's a Marine, I slowly turn my head, as to not create any detectable movement. It is Gy/Sgt Pazorski, he's moving my way, on forearms and knees. Turning back to keep watch on my zone, which he would give me a hard time about, if I wasn't, I do my thing until he arrives, a few moments later.

As he arrives, he moves up next to me and puts his hand to his head, thumb at his ear, little finger at his mouth. He also mouths the words, with no sounds escaping them, "Put me in touch." My pack next to me, I flip open the top and reaching in, locate the knob from memory and turn it on, slightly. The goal is to wake it up, not anybody else that might hear it. We tend to keep it off until we need to check in, or have something to report. There's always someone on the other end, sitting in a communications tent, or plane, just waiting for a call in from units in the field around the world. Not one to sit inside waiting, I'm glad to be here in the field, as I'm opposed to an air-conditioned tent, or plane, somewhere. I know, what's the difference, right? I'm outside, that's the difference. Here at least, there are things to watch, other than walls. What other job in the Marines can I sneak in wildlife watching, without shirking my duties? After all, *"If it moves, identify it."*

I pass the handset to Gy/Sgt Pazorski. He keys the handset a couple times, I hear no sounds coming from my pack. He shakes his head. Reaching in, I turn it up a little, he keys the set and this time, both he and I hear a little static. Talking in a low voice, he communicates with the folks at home. One of the things we're taught is, whispers actually travel farther than talking in a low calm voice. So, he does the latter. So low, that I barely hear him, in fact. I keep the watch on my area of responsibility, staying true to my desire to not be in the know. Although, if I'm being honest, I know that I know… everything. It all registers in my brain. I just file it into my subconscious, in lock boxes. Tiny little boxes, never to be opened, even under torture.

When he's done with the handset, he hands it back to me and moves in a little closer, speaking into my ear, "He might be here, we'll wait until dark, and then go for a look see," he says to me. I nod and give him no other reaction. Inside I'm like, who's here? Maybe I should have been listening! Wait, we're going to sneak into a village at night? Cool! I mean, WHOA, seriously, this is craziness. One of the things we trained for, sure, but, seriously? I'm going to get my first opportunity to sneak around a strange village, undetected, at night? Well, at least here, and while in the Marines. We did plenty of that back home, either late at night avoiding the cops, so they don't harass us, or to not be seen by someone's parents, or because we were all hopped up on drugs and paranoid about being caught, the list of reasons go on.

But here, in a place we're not at, in a village that no one I know, knows it even exists. This might be my first opportunity to truly disappear. "Shut the fuck up," I say to myself, in my head. Those voices will get you killed! I don't even know if I get to go in, or if I'll be on the overwatch, with the night vision scope. Although stealth is one of the things I'm good at, one of the things I excelled at in training, moving undetected and hiding. I was only found once, and that was by Gy/Sgt Pazorski, of course.

When he found me, he said, "I knew this is where you would be, it's the best spot, and no-one else would think of it." Unfair advantage, for sure, or just experience and training perhaps?

That night, around 0230, we start our approach. I'm indeed going in! My second mission, and I get to sneak into a village full of live people, for a look see! I'm paired up with Sgt. Cowen, who, even out here, smells a little bit like Skoal Classic. I'm sure he puts a tiny little bit in his lip, from time to time, to keep him up, and his hands, shake free. He's so addicted to it, he would probably smell like that tobacco, a year after his death. I'm happy to be paired up with him, he's been in the green machine for a long time, and would probably be a Gunny himself, if he didn't like to pick fights in bars so much. He's one that will seek out the toughest bully in the bar and pull him, with minimal resistance mind you, into a fight. You see, Sgt. Cowen is like most other Marines, average in stature, and unimposing when he wants to be. He merely bumps into the bully, and within a minute or so, the bully is down, bleeding on the floor! It is fun to watch, albeit bad for our reputation.

We move in silence, and as per usual, the team splits into two's, rarely is any member of the team totally on their own, by policy. There's safely in two's, for many reasons, one of those, is to have each other's back; two brains are as good as three in instant decision-making; and the character of Marines increases with a witness and fellow participant; and the moral support of having a buddy there with you, far outweighs just knowing there's one nearby. Camaraderie while taking on the world alone, is mandatory.

I follow Sgt. Cowen as we move down the hill. Pairing off, we spill around the village in different directions, one team stays at our previous overwatch, to keep an eye on things from above. They also possess our only night vision scope. Another team makes their way around to the far side of the village. Gy/Sgt Pazorski and Cpl. Zinger make their way to the corner of the wall, near the west entrance of the village, which is the only entrance. Their goal, is just this side of the west entrance, literally around the corner.

We're headed to the backside of the village, the opposite of the other entry team. Our goal is to find a target that Military Intelligence believes to be in this, or one of the other villages in the area. The target moves around this area to escape detection, not from his own government, but, from ours. Apparently, he's a hero to some, and a zero to others. It all depends on what side of the drug war you're on. American people supply the demand, and yet, are not the target of the drug wars, the suppliers are. Unfortunately to some, the suppliers are the hero's, supplying jobs, money, and food, to those who's governments have failed them. Years of catering to their 1%, has created lots of dissidents and a willingness to protect the suppliers, being grateful for the income and protection they provide. And from the CIA's perspective, drug suppliers are either friend or foe, depending on the winds of change, sometimes they're encouraged and protected, other times they're hunted like dogs. Apparently, this guy has found himself in the hunted dog category. Again, mine is not to reason why.

We've worked our way to the village wall, luckily the village's water supply, a gentle river, is on the other side of the village, so no water crossing is necessary. We sit just inside the brush line, hidden under the canopy for a few minutes, looking up and down the line of the wall. There's a trail that runs about five feet out from the wall. I'm sure it goes from the front entrance, all along the wall and into the transition zone, beyond. The trail is evidence that there's not a used gate out the back side of the village. We all know in our heads, that if this is really a hide-out for someone, there's a high chance of a second exit from the compound somewhere. It would be great to know where that is, before going in and flushing him out.

I lean in to speak to Sgt. Cowen, "How 'bout we go to the backside of the village, to see if there's a secret escape?" he looks at me inquisitively. Squishing his face, he shakes his head. Thinking of me as all the rookie that I am, he dismisses my suggestion, purely on principal. Pointing at a spot on the wall, he signals that he is going to go first, and I am to follow. Nodding my agreement, I move on from my suggestion and get ready to cover him with my eyes. The area around the wall, being nearly free of most vegetation, will make him look like a big green cicada on the wall, good thing it's dark as can be tonight. Even with my night vision, it'll take effort to see more than 15 feet to either side of where he'll be, on the wall.

He starts off in a crouch, so low he's no taller than when he was sitting here, while he was reconnoitering the area. Reaching the wall, Sgt. Cowen is up and over, before I have a chance to look in both directions. I heard not a sound from him, or from either direction; listening for a moment more, I attempt to hear some noises coming over the wall that would   signal his detection. Nothing.

I make my move, and attempting to leave no visual profile I travel as low as possible to the ground, all the duck-walk punishments from training paying off. Between the hours of duck-walking between the bulkhead and center of the barracks with a scrub brush, strengthening the legs, and the fact that I'm radio free (*It was left with the overwatch above, since they can see all, it would be up to them to call in on the radio, if all hope is lost*). I move with minimal effort in this crouched position, my back parallel with the ground, head and eyes up, scoping what's in my view, between the ground and the underside of my boonie cover. My legs never stop, as I make my way across the short distance between the line of brush and the wall.

As I approach, I take a closer look at the wall. It's about 6' tall and made out of the local limestone, mostly dry fit, with the occasional mud glop filling in random large spaces. It seems well made, and will hold my weight without falling apart, or making a noise. As I was trained to do, I leap up, grabbing the top, placing my rifle there, and with my other hand, I wrap my arm around it to prevent anyone located on the other side, from grabbing it. A millisecond later, I'm laying flat on top of the wall, rifle still protected. I take a wide look into the village and jump down. It's farther than I expected, a good 8-to-9 feet. I land hard! My knees rush to my face. Engaging the muscles, I prevent chin and knee contact, but, an electric shock zings its' way up my left leg, from the ground to my brain. A pain, large and incapacitating, travels from my foot up into my receptors. What the hell! I grimace.

In my hurry, I forgot to look down, as I released myself from the wall, I hadn't noticed that there was a couple of feet difference, between the inside of the wall and the outside, and because of this, I had landed wrong. Standing there on pause, I notice Sgt. Cowen in the shadow of the wall, looking at me like, "What? Why are you standing there like an idiot?"

Moving, I join him in his crouch. There's definitely something up with my foot. Something extra found its' way inside, the pain is excruciating. I'll need to get it out, just as soon as possible. Maybe I landed on something and I jammed it way up through the boot sole, and then inside my foot. I instantly regret switching the crape soles of my jungle boots with a Vibram mud lug. It's a great sole for the boot, but, I had the cobbler take out the cold and heavy protective steel shank in the boot, when he put the new soles on.

Sgt. Cowen is glaring at me, he's thinking I'm in one of my daydreams. I look down at the boot sole and find nothing protruding in or out of it. Moving my foot around, I can feel it is not pinned to my boot. Hmm, interesting. I lean into Sgt. Cowen, "I did something to my foot."

He gives me the WTF look again, shrugs his shoulders and mouths, "Well?" Basically, just wondering if I'm ready to continue. I nod my head. Mission first, morale second, let's do this. We work our way through a sleeping village. Not sure what I'm to look for, I basically follow Sgt. Cowen, while he looks for signs of someone important; dogs, guards possibly, or just a bigger house.

I'm pretty sure I was picked to search the village, not because of my experience, but, because I'm really good at moving around, undetected. Hell, I've been known to make myself disappear in a room full of people, to say nothing about when I'm in stealth mode! I move silently behind Sgt. Cowen. We spend more time listening and observing from the shadows, than in moving. Hugging walls and dark spots, we work the village from one wall to the other, avoiding the big open space in the center. I begin wondering where I would live, if I could pick my spot in the village. Being of the quiet, behind the scenes type, I would find a quiet corner, surrounded on two sides with a wall, and the houses around me would either be empty, or full of my most trusted.

Who knows about this guy, no-one told me anything, to say nothing about his personality type. Based on all the movies I've seen, whoever's in charge would be located in the biggest house, on the edge of the town square. Not my spot, but, then again, I'm not a bad guy in the movies. We pause for movement on the other side of the square, something is in the shadows. Two somethings. They appear to be green, such as ourselves. After a long pause on both sides, a sliver of a red light appears across the square from the shadows. Sgt. Cowen has his moonbeam out and returns the sliver of red light, for a brief second.

While I sit and wait whatever is next, my foot takes the opportunity to throb incessantly. It seems to be in cahoots with my heartbeat, they move with the same pace. Something is most definitely up with my foot. I'm just hoping it's not too bad. If they have to evacuate me, then the mission is likely over, for all. I do not want to be the reason the mission is scrapped.

The other team makes their way over to our position, working their way slowly, they take notice of everything on their way over. After arriving, Sgt. Cowen and Gy/Sgt Pazorski lean ear-to-ear, to catch up on the fun and frolic of the last hour or so. Cpl. Zinger and I face to the outboard, to watch and listen. I resist the urge to close my eyes and just listen, knowing that can lead to a quick deep rest. This is not the time for that! Letting my eyes glaze over, I watch for movement and let my ears wake up to the sounds around us. No movement is heard, even the village dogs are sleeping at this ungodly hour. 0400 is a prime sleeping time, for all living beings not of the nocturnal persuasion.

Any later, and the bladders of old folks will need to be emptied, and the early risers will start their day. This is the perfect time for a look-see in a place you have no idea what you're looking for, or, at least, I don't.

Sgt. Cowen comes back over and talks in my ear, "We're getting out of here, Gunny doesn't think he's here. You and I are checking the last area on the far side of the compound, it seems neither group checked it, then we're jumping back out of here," he says.

I nod my head. The throbbing in my foot is messing with me, I'm ready to be on the move again. I didn't feel anything when we were active, perhaps then my brain is occupied with more important things than pain.

We move off to check the last area of the village, it's in an odd location off to one side. This is where I would be, I say to myself. Sgt. Cowen does not seem to agree, and we head for the wall closest to where we are. This time, he sends me first. Since this wall's about 8' tall, I'll have to really stretch to reach the top, and I decide to sling my rifle over my back. I make my quiet leap, using my good foot, and I gain the top. Laying across the flat surface, I hear nothing, but, the gentle river that flows next to the village on that side. I drop down and wait for Sgt. Cowen to make an appearance. He does momentarily, and we head, undetected, to our rendezvous at our original overwatch location.

Gathering together, there's a new excitement in the air, there always is, when the team gathers back up. Silently, glad we are all OK, unable to pat each other on the back, and knowing we are not done with our mission anyway, we show our teeth to each other, in a brief glowing smile, and then refocus, while we wait for whatever is next. Watching L/Cpl Alvarez close his mouth and go green again, is a cool thing to see, such is how well our issue grease paint and our camouflaged fatigues work. I know he's right there, and yet, for a second after his mouth went closed, I could not see him. My eyes had to adjust to the concept of seeing his outline again, after the contrast of his teeth.

Gy/Sgt Pazorski and Sgt. Cowen are in a convo (*conversation*). I make my way over to Cpl. Zinger, he fulfills the medical duties while we're on a mission without a proper doc. I lean in and talk to his ear, "I think I fucked up my foot," I say.

"How so?" he asks back.

"It's throbbing and it felt like I was electrocuted," I say.

He looks at me inquisitively, "Let me see it."

I bend down and remove the square knot holding my bootlace tied. I realized early on, that the square knot is far superior than a traditional bow tie, or even a doubled one. Simple and strong, it's my go-to knot, for keeping my things under duress tied and where they need to be. Unwrapping the extra lace and then loosening the boot so I can pull my foot out takes some real effort, it seems my lower shin is expanding as I give it room. I decide to just yank out my foot, while holding the jungle boot securely with both hands. That turns out to be excruciatingly painful. Succeeding in removing it from the boot, I present the foot to him; it seems to be growing, as I watch it. Cpl. Zinger grabs my foot and starts to feel around with his hands. Before we know it, Gy/Sgt Pazorski is in our faces.

"Put that boot back on Marine!" he says, "What are you doing taking it off now?" he demands, looking at Cpl. Zinger.

"I think he broke it," Cpl. Zinger says in reply. Cpl. Zinger chooses that moment to push his thumb down on the top of my foot. If there was a roof, I would have hit my head on it. That's how high I involuntarily jumped. The amount of pain surprised me and it was more than I could suck up in surprise.

Looking back at me Gy/Sgt Pazorski says, "Put it on now, and lace it up tight. Quickly."

I squeeze the foot back into the boot, it's harder this time, the foot is swelling. Even with putting the boot on the ground and pushing, it still takes some effort to get my foot flat to the plastic mesh insole, it takes my weight and the ground pushing back, to do so. The pain, … well, the pain threshold is pretty high. I'm now forcing my foot into an object that, although it held it a few moments ago, the foot is now at least two inches bigger in circumference, than it was when I removed it. After succeeding, I pull the laces as tight as I can and wrap the extra lace around the top of the boot, and tie my simple square knot. Wow! The realization sinks into me and GySgt Pazorski, who was watching the process, that my foot is broken.

Gy/Sgt Pazorski has his head in his hands, he's looking at the ground. Looking up, his eyes hold a question…. *"Am I hurt bad enough that we have to scrap the mission, or can I Marine through it?"* It will be about 20 years, before I learn not to Marine through it, so, I respond to his unasked question.

"I'm good to go, Gunnery Sergeant," I say. He looks at me, grateful I think, knowing I'm putting the mission first. It saves him from a hard call; scrapping the mission would be a failure. We will go on.

22

I spend the next few days walking from village to village. When on the move or active, the pain is constant, therefore, easier to block out. When I'm at rest, or my mind is, then the throbbing is relentless. Needless to say, the throbbing prevents any real sleep!

At the third village, I'm tired of being on overwatch. Gunny's doing the best he can to keep my movement to a minimum. He puts me on overwatch at every village, the repetition quickly bores me, and gives the foot plenty of time to throb. I would prefer to be active and on the move, in order to be distracted from the pain, but, I'm sure, not adding miles is best. All I would need to do is let the pain get to me once, hesitate just for a second, and one of us gets dead, so, I understand the decision. Although I don't appreciate the time spent counting the space between throbs, I do enjoy overwatch.

I like being able to watch nature go by, and to spend time listening to the sounds around me, trying really hard to hear what is not there, amongst the nature sounds.

Human footsteps, or talking. I must hear that, if it happens. So far, life is perfect, not even one human has approached, no critters have screeched at me, or charged me even. I've heard war stories about being charged by tigers, or apes, or bitten by snakes, shit like that. There are many more tales about calm interacts with the locals though. Snakes crawling over a prone body, bees landing on noses and coming to hang out on stationary Marines. I would say we're doing something right, if the wildlife trusts us enough to come hang out with us. Non-threatening to the core.

The breeze sows its' essence within my nostrils, I smell perfume, can't be, must be the actual flower itself. I don't have the words to describe what I'm feeling, I mean smelling. Perhaps, it smells like that girl I really liked in high school. The one with heavy metal t-shirts, glossy lips, and teased up hair, that smelled like Aqua-net. She wore several different perfumes purchased from the drug store, not all at once, she cycled through them until she found the one I liked, and then stuck to it. It wasn't until one day, when I was daydreaming in the field, that I realized that.

This smell wasn't all chemicals like those were though, this smell is real. My young and focused warrior mind is unable to come up with descriptives. Let's just say it smells like comfort, hair spray, lotion, and innocent pussy.

23

I hear movement in the brush, off to one side, and a little lower than my position. The noise is slow, like something that's moving, attempting to make no noise. I look over at Cpl. Zinger, he's heard it as well. He nods slightly, and then turns back to keep an eye on his field of responsibility. I place my eyes near where I think the sound is coming from. Keeping them stagnant, I attempt to see movement, holding my eyes still. I pick out Sgt. Cowen working his way over to us.

"We found him," he says. I still wonder who "him" is! Whoever he is, he's important enough for us to spend time wandering around looking for him.

"OK," I respond.

"Gunny needs you to set up a hasty extract. We're going to get him out of here, as soon as possible. We need to pick a spot. I'll go back down and pass the word," he says.

I smile. This will be fun! "OK," I say, and reach for the handset radio, lying within reach. Then, I pause, "Wait, do you have a map? I don't."

Sgt. Crabtree, reaching into his chest pocket, grabs the map folded there. He puts it down in front of us and points at the clearing, where the village is. "This is the village," he says, "And…" I note the coordinates of the village, and also determine our relation to it.

"This is us," I say, pointing just up the northern hill. We have a perfect vantage point of this village, no sun behind us to cast any shadows, and because of the tough terrain, there are no trails or casual wanderings from the villagers below.

Our only concern would be some sun reflection off of our gear, which we're adamant about keeping shine free, taped, and black. I continue, "This is us here, and the only other clearing I see nearby, is either up on the hill behind us, or the next one is a few miles away. Do you see another one that's usable?"

He looks at the terrain the map he holds. It's full of limestone cliffs, thick jungle, and waterfalls.   Not much in the way of big clearings, or any clearings, for that matter. For a hasty extraction, we need a 50-foot clearing, we can do it in less, but, 50-foot is a good safety margin. It gives the helicopter pilot some leeway, and with an unwilling passenger below, a little leeway is a good idea.

I think back to an incident in training on Camp Lejuene. We were teamed up with the helicopters that day, practicing pick-ups and drops-offs. One of my favorites, is the long rope extraction SPIES Rig, the team dons harnesses with carabiners at our center point. The helicopter comes down with ropes already dangling, we hook our carabiners to them and put our arms around each others' shoulders as he lifts us off the ground. There's also a single rope version, where we're strung out like bait on a fixed fishing line. The feeling is that of a roller coaster, as it forces you to its' will, with the G-forces in random directions. It always takes the pit of my stomach a little longer to leave the ground, than the rest of me. It's a moment of high adrenaline, as we secure ourselves to each other and the pilot rises to a cruising altitude above the trees. Once we've traveled the required distance, he sets us down again. This part takes lots of practice for the pilot, and it isn't always easy to trust them. Part of the job, I guess.

On this training day though, one of the helicopter jockeys was having a rough day. He blew his liftoff, or was being a wise ass, whichever I'll never know, and he commenced moving forward with the Marine's attached below, traveling a mere five feet above the ground. Before he gained necessary elevation, he bounced the group of tied-in Marines against a big, green dempsy dumpster. *CLAAANG*, is a sound I will never forget, it reverberated through my eardrums. Part of me wonders why it was only one sound, not a multitude of impacts. Although, I do think I remember the sound of the dumpster sliding a bit, as well. Perhaps it was the speed of the helicopter, it's my brain tuning out what happened, after the initial sound. I knew it was going to happen. I was watching, as most of us do when in training. We take turns grab-assing and messing with each other, as we wait for our turn. Until a chopper comes in for a lift off that is, then we all pause what we're doing to watch and see how the Marines getting lifted do. Like lots of us humans, we're waiting for an inevitable cluster fuck, by a group.

Succeed or fail, we were open to both, although we were rooting for a screw up, so we could raz them for months about not being able to clip on, or getting hung upside down, or a chopper pilot jerking them off the ground. But, that day was different. Gasps and expletives escape the mouths of the Marines watching. There will be no jabs or ribbing of those Marines, they will be sent home, either in body bags, or with a permanent disability. I never did hear good scuttlebutt, as to which. I did hear that the helicopter pilot and co-pilot were assigned blame for the incident, and sent separately, to parts un-known. Whenever a Marine is instrumental in killing, or in gravely injuring Marines, they're sent to the far gates of Hell, to serve out the rest of their service time. The intent is to protect, as much as it is to punish. We just don't take very well to someone's negligence, leading to the death of our brethren. The removal of the culprit, is as quick as the evacuation we're about to perform.

Sgt. Cowen and I both look up at each other, the questions leaving our faces, we both come up with the idea, simultaneously. "The village," he says first.

I nod, "The village. We do it directly from the village."

"It's the biggest space, and this way, we don't have to fight anyone off while we attempt the extraction. We extract him directly from a roof in the village, and then E&E our way home," he says.

I make the call, informing base that we have their man and we would like to do a hasty extraction from a roof in the village. We receive a *"wait one"* from the voice on the radio. I'm sure he's waiting for those decision-makers in the command center, to go over our suggestion and make some decisions. Here's hoping they like our plan; it is the safest!

"Tiger two, Tiger two, do you copy."

"This is Tiger two. We copy. Over," I reply.

"This is Tiger one, Tiger two proceed with your plan. Be ready

for a hasty at O-eight hundred. Do you copy?"

"This is Tiger two, hasty at O-eight hundred. We copy. Over," I say, and then turn the radio back off. I'll turn it on again, close to the liftoff time. My consolation prize is, I get to man the radio, and watch the show from here. Not as fun as forcing someone into a harness and watching the look on their face when they lift off, but, it still beats a day inside.

24

Cpl. Zinger and I haven't heard or seen a sign of the rest of the team since Sgt. Cowen had disappeared into the bushes. It's ten minutes to forced extraction time, so I turn on the radio, keeping it low just in case, we wait for the radio to come live, or to see something below. The radio grabs our attention first.

"Tiger two, Tiger two, this is Tiger one. Over."

I pick up the handset and press in the button, "This is Tiger two, go ahead. Over."

"This is Tiger one. The short bus is inroute and on time. Are we good to proceed?"

Cpl. Zinger and I look at each other. He shrugs his shoulders. **"I have no idea!"** is what I want to shout into the handset. Who's idea is it, to always ask that question? How the Hell would I know? Don't you think this grand country called the United States could afford to send us in with more than one radio! What the fuck!?!

"This is Tiger two. We are ready for pick up. Do you copy? Over," I say into the hand-piece.

"This is Tiger one. We copy. Over."

What else was I supposed to say? Um, sir. I haven't seen

or heard anything from the team in a couple of hours, so, I have to assume everyone is OK, and they have the package, or a plan to grab the package at the very last minute, but, I really don't know! **NOT.**

Cpl. Zinger and I watch the village below intently, as they flow through their natural morning routine. He points to one of the larger structures in the village, there's some action on the roof. Off to one corner, I see two Marines. At this distance, it's hard to know exactly who, but, my best guess is Gy/Sgt Pazorski and Sgt. Cowen. They lean over and lift something up together; it appears to be someone tied up and blindfolded. Legs and hands bound, they have to move the package as if it were a piece of meat. And this, they do with ease. Once on the roof, they hunker down and wait. One of them, I think Gy/Sgt Pazorski appears to be looking in our direction. I'm tempted to signal him in Morse Code, using the sun's reflection, but, at this point, why risk giving away my position. He'll have to wait for the helicopter noise. I look at my watch, it reads 0757. It's then, that the radio crackles to life, albeit, quietly.

"Tiger two, Tiger two. This is the short bus. Do you copy? Over."

I like this guy! Who in their right mind would want their call sign to be "short bus". Somebody who, if they weren't an officer, I would have drinks with. Not that I have an issue with officers, but, fraternization is forbidden. Besides, grunts and pilots don't mix, as a rule.

"Short bus, Short bus, this is Tiger two, we copy."

"Tiger two, this is Short bus. Are we a go for a hasty?"

"Short bus, this is Tiger two. We are a go for a hasty. Big square building with the flat roof, sir. They're ready and waiting. Over."

"Tiger two, Tiger two. We copy, over."

I can barely pick out the sounds of the chopper approaching. He'll be low and just over the tree tops, out of both radar and any line of sight. He'll no doubt appear at the last second and swoop down into the village where, having just heard the sounds of the approaching helicopter, Gy/Sgt Pazorski and Sgt. Cowen are standing up their package. The package is still blindfolded and the hands are tied behind his back. They cut the binds at his ankles in order to put on a harness. He doesn't struggle. He's either groggy, unconscious, or has submitted to his fate. They pull the harness up to his groin and stand him up. He appears to stand on his own, as they finish the harness. Able to put it on without untying his hands, he stands there, blind in his fate.

The chopper sounds come from everywhere now, the sounds reverberate off the cliff face behind us. The helicopter appears close to our position, off to my left. I see a Marine standing in the door of the ancient door-less helicopter, he's harnessed and standing there with rope in his hand. The hook is already in position, out the side of the open doorway.

I also see a civilian man. He has hair feathered back over the ears, which tells me he is not a military man. The man's holding on to the seat's metal support tube with one hand, while attempting to look through some binoculars with the other. Wearing a Hawaiian shirt, blue jeans and comfortable shoes, he's an anomaly in the helicopter.

As they swoop into position, the Marine in the helicopter throws down the rope. It dangles 50 feet below, the weight holding it as taunt as possible. The pilot lowers the chopper to a perfect distance and moves in closer to the three humans standing on the roof. The Marines on the roof hustle their package over to meet the rope.

The village comes alive as the show ensues. All are out and wondering what's up. Well not all, a few are grabbing M-16's and preparing to fire. American made rifles, hmm, that's very strange, but, not a big surprise to me, as I think about it. Gy/Sgt Pazorski and Sgt. Cowen quickly hook the man in, as a few rifle shots are heard. Once the man is attached, they move over to the back edge of the building, as Sgt. Cowen circles his arm rapidly over his head, letting the chopper know their package is ready. Instantly, the chopper rises and starts hoisting their package into the helicopter.

The rifle shots stop quickly. Apparently, they're smart enough not to shoot at their own boss. We all watch as the man is hauled up into the helicopter by a speed winch, as the pilot simultaneously zips away from the village, towards us, with intentions to disappear over the hill.

I get a quick close-up of the man as he's hauled the final distance into the chopper, his blindfold has blown off, his eyes bulge out of his head, showing the unseen backs of them, his eyebrows are leaping off the top of his forehead and his mouth is showing his tonsils. I can't say I would ever recognize him, such is how quick was the look I got. I'll never forget the look on his face.

As I look down, I watch the rest of the team melt into the shadows, the village swarms, armed men appear, and it's time for us to go. Cpl. Zinger and I put our packs on and move, low and slow, toward our rendezvous point. Once there, we'll escape and evade as necessary, and when it's safe to do so, radio Tiger One for our ride home.

The throbbing in my foot subsides, as my body comes

into motion and the pain becomes constant, I hope our extraction point is not too far, we've been out in the field for two weeks now. My foot gave way on the second day; at this point, I'm curious as to its' physical state. The pain says it's bad.

Cpl. Zinger and I meet up with Gy/Sgt. Pazorski and Sgt. Cowen, and within minutes, the other two team members, arrive. "No signs of pursuit Gunny," Cpl. Alvarez reports in.

"Hmm," is Gy/Sgt Pazorski's only response, as he puts out his hand for the horn. I grab it from its' handle as I ponder why. Why would they not put all hands on deck, to rescue their leader? Perhaps they're incompetent, scared, and fearful. Maybe he's a dictator and they're happy he's gone. Or ponder this, you're a villager, living in the middle of the jungle, you're sleeping soundly. Knowing your leader is in the village, you're safe, protected vicariously by his men. Then one morning, you're awakened from your contented slumber by a horrendous noise in the sky. You rush outside, and through hazy eyes that are bashed by dirt, you see your great leader disappearing into the sky, as if snatched by your god in anger. Maybe you would not pursue either. Instead, you go inside and give thanks that he did not choose you that day. *WHAPP.*

Gunny smacks me in the head with the handset, "Here Marine." He no longer takes offense to my daydreaming moments, instead, he enjoys bringing me back to the now.

"You'll be happy," he smiles at me. Is that gratitude I see in his eyes? "They're going to extract us from the top of that hill." He points behind me.

Sgt. Cowen grabs the back of my neck before I can

148

turn and look, "You did good Marine," he says quietly in my ear, "When we get back, we'll send you off to the medical center, and we'll see how you do there." He smiles mischievously at me.

We reach the hill with no worries, and wait with double checked harnesses on, until we hear the helicopter approaching. Still in quiet mode, sure we're undetected, one Marine creates a motion target, while Gunny confers on the horn with Tiger One. Tiger One confirms with the pilot that we are in the required position, then Gunny confirms, yes, that is us you see on the hillside, please don't shoot us. No rockets either, thank you.

The rope is lowered from the helicopter to us. We all click in with our carabiners, two each, and relax our bodies for the ride. Every time I do this, that incident in training comes to my mind. The incident doesn't matter in the big scheme of things. Death is a part of this job; the clicker in my head keeping the death count, tells me we are at 200. Well, I am, who knows how many deaths the more senior members of the team have experienced. I close my eyes to the wind on my face. I feel free, dangling from the giant motorized mosquito, the air dries the jungle's moisture from my body, searing through my clothes, it steals the sweat for its' own humidity. I don't care, I'm done with it. Enjoying this feeling, I am distracted, as my body's blood floods to my feet, doing its' damnedest to use my broken foot for a bass drum. It has me wondering if I am done. Two missions in, and I might be done with the teams, with the Marines Corps even.

25

Needless to say, I don't receive good news at the medical center, my aching foot is indeed broken. Doc informs me it probably started as a stress fracture in one of the metatarsals, and it compounded from there. Five broken bones (three of them metatarsals) and a fallen arch, are the grand totals. A striking blow to the integrity of the foot's function.

Six months later, I'm faced with a choice: ride a desk, or take an honorable medical discharge. I contemplate my choices. The arrogant bravado part of me thinks the discharge is better than riding a desk. Using the fear of being an office 'pogue' as an excuse to escape more death, when facing the Physical Evaluation Board, I chose the honorable medical discharge. Although my final memorable experience with the beloved Corps, does not make this decision feel honorable.

Before my paperwork goes through, I have one more Friday morning inspection. The captain in charge of the medical platoon (a holding platoon for those in flux, due to injury, or mental issues) insists on keeping us busy, this is still the Marine Corps, after all.

C.M. Halstead

We all have jobs around the base. Every Thursday evening, is a complete barracks cleaning, complete with an inspection of each Marine and the barracks, every Friday morning at 0730. For most of these inspections, we wear our inspection BDU's, sometimes Class B's. Either way, the clothes we wear are only worn for the inspection period, and then they get returned to the wall locker, until the next inspection. The same goes for the boots or shoes. They're shined, polished and returned to perfection, then they're placed in the Marine's inspection position, and there they wait, until the Marine steps into them, the next morning for inspection.

Apparently, just before my last inspection, the Captain hears that I'm getting out. His beloved Corps has a Marine who is quitting, his anger becomes apparent, to all in the medical platoon, at the beginning of the inspection.

I had managed to grab a rack at the far end of the squad bay. With no one sleeping above me, a wall with a fire door on one side, and a Marine on the top bunk next to me, it's as close to privacy as I can obtain, in quarters like this. My wall locker contains all my inspection requirements, I triple checked, a few moments ago. Everything was there, and no changes were made, except to realign each item. Pass or fail, was the difference between doing whatever the Hell I wanted this weekend, or extra duty. I have never failed an inspection, nary a ding each week, so, there are no worries on my mind. There's always something they mention, continuous improvement, and all that.

Some days the Captain starts with the Marine closest to the door and slingshots his way around the squad bay, until he's done. Other days, he walks down to the end, my end, and he works the room from one end to the other. Today, he heads straight for me. He stops dead in front of me and plants his feet. The platoon Sergeant, beelines for my wall locker. The Captain looks me dead in the eye and makes a *tsk* sound, as he curls his lip. No emotion on his face, yet, extreme anger in his eyes.

"How's it look?" he asks the 1st Sergeant.

"Ahem," escapes the 1st Sergeants lips.

The captain leans around the wall locker's door for a peek, nodding his head he says one word, "Unsatisfactory." And leans back to attention, looking me in the eye, "I heard you're quitting, taking the P.E.B."

"Yes, sir," I reply.

Disappointment crosses his face.

The First Sergeant pulls out a perfectly pressed pair of Class B trousers, holds them up for a second, inspecting them, then he drops them to the floor. He reaches in for the second pair, drops them to the floor. He takes my dress blue blouse, holds it, and returns it to hang, just about everything else he removes from its' designated position. Including the never worn, tighty-whities, black, green and white socks. T-shirts, the BDU's.... Everything finds its' way to the floor.

He goes around to my footlocker, removes the trays, dumping the contents onto the floor, after throwing the empty trays onto my rack, he dumps the footlocker upside down. The Captain holds my attention and his military bearing perfectly, as do I, while the First Sergeant has his way with my gear. The message is clear.

When the First Sergeant comes back online, next to his Captain, the Captain says to me, quietly, "Quitting is contagious, and everything contagious, must be isolated."

I had no idea, in that moment, that the feelings of betrayal and the message being given, would haunt me for years to come. All the trials and tribulations, and the strength that they had provided, tainted by this two minutes. Two minutes was all it took, to teach me I was a failure in the eyes of my beloved Corps.

Guilt.

      Shame.

            Disappointment.

                  Not glory, are the final messages.

      Fuckers.

26

Walking off the plane and up the portable walkway, I slow my pace to meet the civilians around me. Telling myself to chill, I look up the kill box that is the gangplank, and out into the airport. Inside are loads more people. They mill and wander about, lost in their complacency. Either busy waiting, or gathering their wits, as they live in their own little worlds.

The first thoughts through my head: *"Shit, if someone pulls a rifle in here, they'll all be dead. Lets see, that guy looks a little freaky, maybe he has weapons hidden under that long trench coat of his. There are 6 exits, and about 400 hundred people located in the area at the end of this airport terminal, too many to keep track of. What's that fucking beeping noise?"* A hurry cart slowly makes its' way through the crowd, as it works rushing four blue hairs to their exit gate.

I hear talking from all directions, the beeping starts again as the driver works his way through, the noise crescendos, roaring, it rumbles inside my head, echoing back and forth, it induces vertigo.

In this moment, I realize I'm frozen on the edge of the carpet, standing in the middle of the isle, by the last row of seats, the other passengers move around me, giving me dirty looks that change to looks of fear, as they see my face.

Angry, I have my war face on. Jaw set, teeth clenched, mean and nasty, I stand there holding my ruck in my right hand, my left clenched into a fist. I stand there, tall and alert, tense and feeling unsure, I look left and right before stepping off the safety of the carpet onto the tile of the main walk-way. I move quickly and stealthily through the crowds, weaving through the little gaps, the nearest exit my goal. I am out of here!

Zipping by the security guards leaning against the walls, I hurry toward the door that I see, about 100 yards beyond the guards. Outside are taxis, pov's, and buses, loading and unloading. Pushing open the door between me and them, I hurry outside to the fresh air.

No taxi is immediately ready for me, I walk across the roadway, through the parking garage, off through the grass and into no-man's land, a buffer zone between the airport and the rest of the world. I work my way away from the airport, as quickly as I can. Seeing a drainage heading under the highway, I proceed toward it. It will take me to the chain store I see, on the other side of the highway. I can get what I need there.

What did I expect... a hero's welcome? I didn't tell any of my old friends I was arriving today, I didn't even tell my family. Everybody else at the airport is oblivious to my trials and tribulations. It's why they make people like me anyway. Keep the chaos at bay, so they can live in bliss. Why would they want to remind themselves of my existence, I would be a reminder of that which I am, here to prevent them from knowing. And like they would believe me. Someone who lives in the utopia of suburbia would never believe what I, my eyes, have seen. They are my visions to keep. My brain's memories to carry. Guess I will carry them off to somewhere else.

Though we walk through the valley in the shadows of death, for although we are the meanest motherfuckers in the valley, we will be gone before you know, not a trace to be seen or discovered... and although you will often wonder if you did smell, or see, or feel us, you will tell yourself you did not, for it is not possible.

The ghosts hiding in the trees could not possibly be there. There's no way they could be watching and observing your every move. For although you feel the eyes, there's no way it could be... could there be?

And although you may never actually know if he was there, to witness what was not to be seen, what should not be. He will never forget what it is, what it was, and what it should never have been. He lives with the guilt of not being able to tell the truth, and having to tell stories. Living somewhere between the truth and fiction... the guilt slowly eating at his soul, his eyes pleading for those that listen, to hear the truth beneath the lies.

Nothing happened. I wasn't there. Bart Simpson bullshit.

20 YEARS LATER

27

The demon says, "You are nothing."

The demon says, "You did nothing."

The demon says, "How could you do nothing? You just watched. Marines are hero's, and saviors, and you just watched..."
"Failure!" It gets closer, "FAILURE!" it screams at me.
"You undeserving son of a bitch!!!" The demon moves in, getting closer to my face. I can smell its' evil breath, "You should've run down there, and done something, you're a failure of a man!"
Its' decrepit face creeps close to mine, and it works its' way slowly to my ear, in order to whisper its' version of sweet nothings to me, the demon's favorite thing to do.
Sitting up suddenly, I awake from my dream. The dream I have at least once each night, and have had, for as long as I can remember. Except, it's getting worse, I can smell him now. The demon, that is.
The demon is right, it's the reason I'm living out here, in the wilds. I don't deserve to live in society, I failed them,

let them down, they expected me to save them all. I wanted to save them all. Instead, we all died.

28

I dive deep down into the depths of my soul. The emphasis worth over emphasizing, how far down inside the wound burns a hole. It smolders slow, a root burning underground, it rises its' fire in odd places, coming to the surface mysteriously, and at will. I could control the shadow, but, I don't want to. Everything after, but, is bullshit.

I let it burn, I deserve to lack an entire soul, only the innocent are whole, and once that innocence is lost, it's impossible to return. Even if it is earned.

29

The two hikers cover ground quickly and effortlessly. I move to put some vegetation between me and the trail. I'm already 20 feet to one side of it, and yet, I take no chances, even after all these years. I move with my back to a Cyprus and lower myself to the ground, back to the tree, with the tree between me and the trail.

I listen as they approach; the first hiker is making good time, not messing around with a conversation, he plods forward with purpose. Based on stride and impact, the hiker seems like a big dude who drives his heels in and pushes against the sand to propel himself forward, moving the earth backwards behind him. This guy's covering ground!

Behind him, comes someone of a light foot. This one's moving sand, not much else. He glides through, using the balls of his feet, he utilizes the earth's turn. Moving quickly and silently, neither of them are the average weekend hiker. Deciding to sneak a peek out of curiosity, I lean my head around the tree, ever so slightly, to get a look at this pair. Or one of them, at least. The first is further down the trail and hidden by the vegetation, the sounds of his heel-digging steps still present.

The second guy is slight of stature, bent over, not from the pack, but, of the weight of the world on his atlas bone, he still glides down a trail, somehow. Turning back behind the Cyprus, just as the hiker turns to look my way, I pause my breath and think invisible. Explains a lot, actually, he is trained. Listening, I hear him lightly move the sand as he flies the contours of the trail. The sounds quickly becoming faint, I resume my breathing.

I smell a cross between skunk and propane. There must be Javelina nearby. Javelina travel in herds, minding their own business, foraging and rooting their way through their square mile territory, unlike the birds and coyote, these pig-like creatures are born and die within that same square mile. They're not travelers by any means, their ancestors long ago grabbed the best territory for their herd and they've been here ever since. Sometimes, human civilization crops up around them and they feast on the spoils of their excess, if it's possible, or move to the shadows if it's a zone patrolled by dogs. Most of their existence is crepuscular, moving about during the times that are hardest to see. Winters have them sunning themselves during the day, and summers have them dog piled in the shade, on the coolest terrain of their homeland. Adaptable in lifestyle and diet, they have been in existence forever, it seems. I've learned a lot from these local creatures, over the last couple of years.

Staying there for a while longer, I close my eyes to listen. Listening to a slight breeze, I hear not much else, the two experienced hikers having moved their way into the canyon and out of my hearing distance, the only clue to their continued passage is the occasional Scrub Jay bird squawking their warning call to all that can hear. Even the Jay's warning sounds fade into the distance quickly, as the hikers move deeper into the canyon.

Loud leaves announce the presence of a beetle, probably one of the many black ones that work the desert floor during the day time. They wander about, minding their own business, unless I get too close, then they do their best to stick their butts up in the air at me, pausing their activities to keep their pointy exterior aimed in my direction. My steps announce my movement to them through the earth. It is the vibrations they're in tune with, more than my shadows.

There will be no beetle butt pointing today, as I sit still, listening to it forage and walk with a loudness, through the dryness of the desert floor.

Suddenly, the Cicadas cry out, quickly ramping up in volume, they announce the arrival of the day's heat, magically starting their chorus, simultaneously. Each aware and in-tune with the earth, they yell their gratitude, or is it anger, at the arrival of the heat.

Not much else to listen to, other than the thunderous silence, loud quiet permeates my eardrums. The Tinnitus humming its' machinery noise in the back left part of my head is the most prevalent, then the warming breezes, the Cicadas, and the ***"not good enough"*** voices in my head. Having enough of that last one, I get up to walk. Deciding not to go deeper into the canyon, I instead move perpendicular to the trail and head for the cliff face, having seen enough humans for one day. Nothing but despair and cruelty to be found with them. At least, out here, it all makes sense.

Feeling like moving my body, I decide to walk about for

a few hours. Working my way up the butte, I meander through its' cracks to go up or down, and its' shelves to wander around at a level with each micro-ecosystem. Each shelf is its' own piece of heaven, maintained in perfect balance, purely by location and isolation. Only when interlopers such as I come through, is it at risk of losing that balance. I'm careful not to disturb. I do pause to stare at it, look at it and to check out its' perfection. Nothing is moving in it right now, just me. It's a living being, on pause, dry, dry as can be, nothing is awake at the moment. It looks like a mass of dead.

A mass of dead that's just waiting to come alive, all it takes is just a little water of life. I reach around and grab my Nalgene bottle. Pouring out ½ of the precious contents, I watch as the dormant microcosms come alive, the brown turns to green as the crypto becomes vibrant, it swells with anticipation, rising to absorb all, it strives to grab up every bit of water as quickly as it can, nary a piece falls to the sandy dirt. When it does, the dirt quickly envelops the drops of water in a protective shield of quartz crystals, none if it shall be allowed to evaporate. It saves it, gathers it, and turns it into mud, albeit for a short period of time, before passing it down through to roots unknown.

I stare at the process, watching each little stage. First the crypto, then on to the mud. My attention draws back to the biotic organisms that appear as mossy-like plants when alive with moisture, as they are now. Awake for a surprising amount of time, I watch the translucent green slowly morph back to its' dormancy, I trance into its' process, only to be unnoticed if I can stay immobile and focused on its' painfully slow transition.

I notice light reflecting off an object in a dry area of the sand. Moving some grains out of the way, I bring it to the surface with a tip of my finger. It is chipped, and worked by human hands. Made of obsidian, it's shiny and sharp, even to this day. This particular one is about ¾ finished, and ¼ natural rock state, an arrowhead. Someone started this and lost it enroute to parts unknown. Rubbing the piece back and forth with my thumb, I hold the arrowhead between it and my forefinger, and watch the drying crypto-biotic soil.

The vibrant green reminds me of another place. Smell the dank, skanky, organic smells of the humid air, I do. Taking a slow deep inward breath through my nostrils, I savor all it has to offer.

I smell rot.

We spent almost all of our training time in North Carolina, a place of very diverse ecosystems, different than this. Dry and sandy, there's not as much smell of rot, as there is here. Interesting that now in a desert, I smell rot more than in the humidity of the southeast. More than anywhere else I can remember. Strange that even I, in this situation, would be daydreaming, but, I will forever be checking out of the current situation.

30

I see movement off in my peripheral. Refocusing, I see a coyote sulk by. Coyote is the trickster, the jokester, the scavenger, the omnivore-ian competition. He lives in our midst, and to most of us, he's unknown. He feeds off our scrapes, and takes our pets, if we're unwise enough to leave them within reach. They do so silently, until they have grabbed some lunch, but then, the coyotes cackle and call to inform us of their victory. They call in their friends, if there is enough to share. The coyotes walk by undetected, just inside the shadows. Our pets let us know, if we are capable of listening. If we can get our attention out of the TV and the other electronic devices long enough, we'll see the dogs and cats go alert, the cats stare out the windows, peaking through the curtains, taunting them, as only a cat is audacious enough to do. The dogs stare through the walls, smelling them walk by, following them with their nose, the coyote either working through the neighborhood, or stalking something under the house.

31

Focusing my eyes, I look down at the ancient arrowhead I found during a rest period, a day or so ago. Rubbing it between my thumb and forefinger, I wonder how long it took for the craftsman to perfect his technique. How many cuts, scrapes, bashed knuckles and fingers did they endure to perfect this little tool of food capturing. How much time, how many years, to perfect it, just to lose it near its' completion.

32

The demon speaks once again in my ear, it whispers its' sweet embrace, "You will never be," it says with glee. "You will never move on." Skanky, nasty, breath on my ear hair. "You will always be with me. You are mine!"

I clamp my palms over my ears, pushing tight to hold out its' verbal onslaught. The demon's weakening speech of truth, its' dire need to punish; it's a necessity for me, the shadow must keep me down, must feed me my beliefs. I deserve none better.

The demon shows itself clearly tonight, deep green are its' scales, an olive drab of sorts. A ghillie suit is created from molting slabs of skin, peeling away at odd angles, causing a near camouflage appearance to its' skins; yellow and gray, the color of years and years of unwashed dirt. Even in the monsoon rains, the demon manages to carry this dirt. The rain hits it, but, does not absorb, it rolls off this armor of dirt with a vengeance. Nothing will get through, it is strong as titanium.

The demon smells of death and destruction. It smells of old blood, and of human wastes of urine and feces. He smells not of fresh and healthy urine, but, of the lost in the desert and haven't had water in days, yet, this nasty, ammonia-smelling brown gel still wants to come out, kinda' smell. The feces is the product of fast-food cheeseburgers and chili cheese fries, mixed with kegs of cheap beer. The odor, all too familiar to those experienced with plywood floor bars and middle of nowhere convenience store outside bathrooms, mixed with the freshly expressed glands of an old dog. Stale, stagnant, tidal saltwater swamps, filled with 1,000-yr-old decaying fish, intermingled with blood and souls of suicidal recruits that were never known, to say nothing about forgotten, who throw their carbon into the mix. Decaying flesh and congealed blood intertwine, offering up the most complete palate of puke inducing, nose lingering stench I could ever hope to inhale into my system.

The demon's voice, raspy and short of breath, running for many a year on nothing, but will, has blown its' lungs of their capacity to process. Musty, moldy, decaying, swamp-filled lungs produce an odor most prevalent to factory farms of pigs and chickens. The smells of the sauerkraut pits and skunks, on 100 degree days, have nothing to compete with the odor expelled with each word he whispers into my being.

"You did nothing, but, watch."

"Some hero you turned out to be."

"Puke." "Maggot." "Scum."

"Cum dripping gutter sluts, are better than you...."

I push my hands tighter on my ears, a yell develops low in my belly, it crescendos and forces its' way through my pipes to the lips, it escapes forcefully, at first only competing with the demon's voice, it soon completely engulfs its' voice, drowning it in sorrow. I fall to my side in despair, finishing my yell with all, but, the minuscule bits of air left in the alveoli of my lungs. Having squelched the voice, I pant for oxygen and lay there, hands still over my ears, I turn toward the sky, focusing on the eternal blue, I regain my breath.

Slowly releasing the grip over my ears, I let outdoor sounds in slowly, the first suction of release induces an ocean of air, followed by the slightly quieter sounds of nature. Sitting up, I decide it's time to return to camp. Finding my way overland organically, I sit down in my favorite spot without realizing it. I stare at the fire pit, a dry cow patty smoldering in the middle holds the embers. I need to bring it up to the cooking levels when I want.

Not sure of what I want, I slide it off to the side and watch the minute glow in the pit, deciding to build it up a bit, I add the necessary ingredients, until I have a good fire to stare into for a while. Always good to get lost into, I look into the ever-mutating orange and red combination. Before I know it, morning will be here. I'm headed into town in the morning. It's supply time, food is scarce. Game is game, but, it's time for a cheeseburger, I can treat myself to that, at the least.

33

I meander, lost in thoughts, an angry buzz alerts me to the poisonous snake's presence, I look around, his camouflage a deterrent to my mission. Spotting him on the edge of a young scrub oak, the snake is, but, a juvenile. The dangerous ones. They'll inject venom every time. Not quite up on the lesson that it's just a waste of venom, he will not be able to eat me, I will kill him in anger, and have a horrible walk into town. Adult rattlers have it figured out. If we get near each other, *rattle, rattle, rattle*, it lets the human know it's there, then the human doesn't step on it. If the human gets really close, bite it and make sure it's paying attention. If the human steps on me or corners me, then its' on. Inject at will, and make it pay.

These are the lessons that come to me, as I meander in my thoughts.

34

I set myself down beneath the under-hang, and out of sight. Always hiding from any interaction with the hikers that come into the canyon, I plan on doing the same with this one entering my proximity.

She is dressed in the usual experienced hiker attire. The skintight yoga pants were left in town, she has on tan hiking pants, light hikers, and good socks. Her shirt is short sleeve and she has a small sun hat on her head, providing shade, but, not so big it'll grab branches as she is scrambling about. She moves fast and steady, having had enough of the trail, she turned off of it, and headed my way a short while ago. Working her way up through the scrub brush, she stops every once in a while to look up above her, she seems to be scanning for a route. I like this woman, she has a plan of attack.

In a short time, I realize her route is going to take her right through where I'm sitting. I wait for my opportunity to move off to the side, where I can put some bushes between her and me. She stops to look up again and I ready myself. As soon as she looks down, I move off to my right. Moving with ingrained stealth, I make my way to a spot about 20 yards away and pause again. From here, I can't see her directly. Closing my eyes and tuning the ears, I hear her moving, light of foot and steadily up the sandstone scree pile, below where I was crouching a moment ago. I take a chance and stay where I am. It's a gamble, if she should decide to go around to the front of the butte at this level, she would go right through where I'm paused on my haunches, waiting to see what she does.

When I had line of sight with her, she seemed to be looking in the opposite direction, like she was going to take that ravine to the next level of rock shelf. I happen to know, that is the closest route up. She doesn't know that, however, and may come this way to explore around the corner. I hear her movements stop while she catches her breath. The sounds of her lungs efficiently grabbing oxygen soften, and then increase, as she turns from looking at the scree located to her right, and turns in my direction.

The Ravens in the sky above announce to all that are listening of her progress up the side of the butte, crooning their distaste at her invasion. How will they steal eggs, if all the mothers are in their nests protecting them, forced there by her presence? The father birds keep a watchful eye on her, as she works her way through their neighborhood, ready to distract her from their mate and impending youngsters locations. I follow her movements using her noise and the local wildlife's sounds as they alert all of their particular species without the human hiker's knowledge.

After a few moments of recovery, she moves off to the right, choosing the visible rock scree. More motivated now that her breath has recovered, she skips the side excursion in my direction for the obvious route. The rocks scraping against each other struggle for purchase, sandpaper to sandpaper, as she pushes upwards off of them. The fingers on the chalkboard sounds repeat themselves, relentlessly. As she defies gravity and moves upwards, the scree is forced a few inches down, making progress to the bottom, surely to make it there some time after, well, sometime.

I hear her gain the next shelf above and take a few heavy steps in this direction on the shelf. From experience, I know there is a thin section, with an enticing area on the other side, that hosts a grandiose view. I know that view will demand she spend some time enjoying it. The thin section is less than a human is usually comfortable with, and it takes a conscious effort for her to commit to the action. I hear her pause and then a rather purposeful foot placement, that, although thoughtfully chosen, still fails.

"Ahh, shit!" I hear above me. Then sounds of tumbling rocks. I hear the rocks clearly off to my side, along the cliff. *"Yep, there they go...,"* I think to myself, as I watch them tumbling down the slippery slope. They bounce, tumble, and break into small pieces as they work their way closer to gravity's source. I hear a bigger rock in motion, or maybe not. Maybe it is her?!?

"Ugh" is the sound that escapes her, when she loses her footing. I hear sliding human for a bit, and then tumbling. Everything goes silent, then a thud, as she hits the ground. I feel the light reaction of the rock beneath my feet. She has fallen off the shelf above, and no doubt landed in the sand and small debris that takes the same path as her.

I can't help myself, I go to see if she's OK. She's lying just around the corner, just my side of the talus pile. She must have tried bailing off the slide, by jumping to the solid slick rock above us. Still a little awake from this morning's rain, the micro-growth, fine when dry, is a slippery type of snot. The desert tapestry sent her careening to her current resting place. The patina has a defense system that kicks in when it is wet, awake, and vulnerable. It used its' greasy slime effect to reject her presence upon it. The hiker gasps again, when she realizes I'm there. I see shock and terror on her face.

"AHHH!" she screams, when she sees me. She uses her hands to pedal herself backward and away from me. I put my hands up in front of me and wave them frantically back and forth.

"No, No, No," I mouth to her, no sounds escaping my lips. The shock on my face apparent, she stops trying to escape. She ceases her movements, and just sits there with her hands palm down on the ground, ready to push again, if need be.

I also squat down on my haunches, trying to make myself smaller, less threatening, I come down to her level, still 15 feet away from her. I make some more reassuring gestures with my hands.

Like two predators coming face to face, we stare at each other for a moment. The first eye contact I've made with another human, for as long as I can remember.

The eyes looking back at me are afraid, and in shock. Mostly from falling off the short cliff and probably more than a little, terrified of me. Suddenly, a realization crosses my brain and I look down at my clothes, noticing their condition. I then see the dirt on my hands and arms. It's warm today, so my layers are back at home base. I'm encased in dry red rock dirt. I can only imagine what my face and hair look like. Grateful to have a hat on, to hide whatever is going on up there, I look up at her, sheepishly.

After a moment, her eyes soften, teary-eyed from the fall or something else, she relaxes. I can't say a smile crosses her face, or anything, but, I can tell she knows I'll not hurt her, and that is what is eminently important.

Not knowing what to say, I switch my hands from palms facing her in reassurance, to my palms up, while I attempt an *"Are you OK?"* gesture. She nods her head and looks at me, inquisitively.

"Can you talk?" she asks. Laughing a little, I nod my head.

"Yeezz" I croak, my voice crackling from lack of use. I try again, "Yes."   Still nodding my head, I hear my real voice for the first time since I last went to town, and then, it was only to tell the cashier, thank you.

"Are you OK?" my voice crackles less this time.

"I'm OK, I think?" she says, then commences to actually check herself out. She has only fallen about 10 feet, and luckily, landed on sand, not a green thing. All green things here poke, prick and stab you. Even the leaves of a scrub oak can give you a wake-up call. She brushes herself off a bit and then decides to stand. I start to stand as well, and then thinking better of it, squat back down on my haunches in order to maintain a less threatening position. She gets up and continues brushing herself off. She is obviously OK, no wincing in pain, as she tries to get every bit of dirt off of herself. Finishing her task, she looks up at me, "Are you OK?" she asks.

I'm taken aback by the question, "Yes, I'm OK, why do you ask? You're the one that just fell off a cliff!"

She laughs, nods her head, "True that! Well, I'm in

luck, I happen to be a nurse, and I can professionally say, I'm OK!"

"Good thing you're a nurse, if you always hike like that!" I say and point up at the cliff she just fell off. I smile for the first time in, forever. It hurts.

She glares at me and smiles simultaneously, creating a perfect grimace. The woman looks at me a bit longer, before she looks away at the view.

She can tell he's been through a lot. It's written in his eyes, whether he knows it or not. She theorizes he doesn't know what he looks like right now, either. Bum-like, is the best way to describe him. Well, maybe not. He's fairly well put together, just dirty as hell, and she can tell from his clothes, that he's been in them awhile. The woman squats down onto his level, also thinking it is best to stay where she is, she keeps her distance and decides to try and engage him from there.

Pointing up above, she asks, "So, anything up there? Any ruins or pictographs or anything? I like to explore around, moved here a few years ago, and I'm just starting to get back here into the back country...." she trails off her ramble. I look at her, not saying anything. She continues, "So far, I've found a few cool things, most things near town are badly disturbed, built on, camped on, and graffitied."

The woman pauses her talking and looks at the homeless man. He is well adorned in outdoor gear, a durable set of hiking pants, a synthetic shirt, and a heavy canvas desert hat. All are earth tone in color, full of said earth, and showing the signs of extended wear, with various needles, thorns, and sandstone scrapes. Obviously, starting to lose the battle, the clothes are all disintegrating in several areas, and are encased in dirt and dust. On his back, is a small military style pack, worn as if he no longer knows it's there.

"Yes," he finally says to her, in reply, "Yes, there are lots of cool things around here."

She smirks, it is obvious he hasn't talked in a while, his speech is hesitant.

"Some are easy to get to, some are not. Most of them are in way better condition than the ones near town. Heck, a lot of the so called ruins near town, have been knocked down and rebuilt on more than one occasion," he says.

"That's cool," she says.

She looks at him again and wonders the last time he spoke to another human being; she watches him fidget for a few seconds. He speaks, "Well, good to meet cha," he says. He turns away from her and departs the scene at a rapid rate.

"Wait!" she says confused, where is he going? She gets up to follow him. Hurrying to catch him, she moves too quickly for someone who just fell off of a cliff. She winces after a couple steps. Her body stiffening from the fall and starting to bruise, she stops her attempt at pursuit. Damn! She was hoping to talk to him a bit longer.

He's in a weird state, yet, there's just something about that guy. She knows what her friends would say, *"It's just your great white savior gene kicking in again. Stay away from him, he's probably dangerous."* Yeah, yeah, whatever, I can take care of myself, bitches. She listens for about a minute and hears nothing. Either he's quiet as a mouse, or he's just out of her sight and waiting for her to leave. She wonders if

179

he's in this area often, she might have to come back here, soon!

Moving swift and silent, I depart from the area where the female hiker fell. Making my way along the cliff-face, I cover the flat ground quickly. Reaching another crack and heading up the butte, expeditiously, I dive into the mini-ravine and work my way up to the next level, then backtrack to a little above where I was just talking to the woman who falls off cliffs. Squatting down in the rest position, I wait for her to move.

I can't see her, yet I know she is below me, a little closer to where I was hiding from her, than where she was when I beat feet, either she's scoping for me or thinking about following me. If she does pursue me, I'll just go down the ravine she scrambled up and make my way out of this area for a while.

She stands there, non-moving for a couple minutes, and then says something that sounds like "fuck it," before turning around carefully, to start her way back down to the trail below. I want to make sure she's really OK, and watch her for a bit to be sure. She's moving gingerly and slow, other than that she seems fine.

I watch until I can't see her anymore and then I squat down into the rest-and-ready stance, listening to her descent. Once she gets to the trail, I hear her speed up a bit. I listen and watch until she's out of sight and hearing distance, which, between this perch, and the sound devoid canyon, means I listened, and sometimes watched her shrinking figure, as she worked her way out of the canyon. About ten minutes after I loose sight of her, I hear a car door close and then an engine start up. She made it.

35

I hear voices entering the canyon on the hiking trail that runs down the center of this canyon. Feeling nosy today, I work my way to my favorite lookout. It gives me the best view of the first mile or so of the trail below, and the dirt parking lot, located on the other side of the unpaved road, that passes in front of all the canyons in the area. Brushing the wilderness area that the canyons host, the road allows access for all types of adventurers.

I recognize one of the voices, it's the woman from the other day, she's back with a friend. Standing just back from the edge, as to not silhouette, I watch them enter the canyon and work their way over to where I met her a week ago. They're taking the same exact route. Watching, it seems the woman is telling her friend the story of her fall. They hang out, extensively, in that area. Even sitting down to talk and eat.

After a while, they stand up and move up to the actual cliff area the woman fell from. I crouch down, now that they're within sight distance. If I can see them, they can see me. It's just how it works.

"Hello!" she calls out. She does this repeatedly. After a

while it becomes so annoying I'm tempted to reply, just to get her to stop it. Eventually, her friend stops her and they head on out, her friend leading. The mystery woman keeps stopping and looking behind her, looking for something. Me. What does she think? I'm a freak show! Screw that. I've been hiding here for years, I will not come out so easy. Does she think I am easy?

36

I stare at the cocoon. It is wriggling in slow motion. If I hadn't been zoning off, I never would have seen the movement. My blurry, unfocused eyes saw the movement and removed me from my haze of thought. Now as I focus, I see everything, every minute detail. The cocoon looks like a cross between a cigar ash and a croissant, two things I have been longing for.

There's this place in town, that makes the best ham, cheese, and spinach croissants. It melts in the mouth, warm and supple, it disappears, more than it's chewed. Two in two minutes, is my post-hike consumption record. I wonder what it would be like now. Maybe four in two minutes.

I inhale deep and slow, feeling the cigar's deep, woody spice enter my nostrils. Somehow, I have a stick between my fingers, and I roll it back and forth. Yep, it's about a . 50 gauge. Bringing it to my nose, it smells like dirt and stick, not what I was looking for. Focusing my attention back on the awakening cocoon, I move just a tad bit closer and take a gander at it, with all the child-like curiosity I can muster.

The ashen shell moves slowly, as the being inside pushes against it. Slow, at first, it becomes translucent, as the sun removes itself from the clouds and illuminates the goings on inside the cocoon. I can see parts of the cocoon being pushed against it, as it cracks from the efforts of the critter inside. The motion is patient, no frantic claustrophobia here. Just the slow progress of nature. The shell cracks as the being inside imparts its' will upon it. Bursting forth, it wedges and worms its' way out, pushing through the small crack, until the cocoon bursts open, unable to structurally resist the transformation.

The fluttering of wings, fast and furious, the moth beats them, vastly swollen in the body, its' wings wrinkled and imperfect. I reach out and gingerly pluck it from its' perch on the branch. Careful not to damage or leave its' legs behind, clinging from instinct. I bring it closer to me, and place it in my other hand. Moving to a sunny spot, I watch the moth do its' thing. The sun, and my palm warm it, the wings power-pump the fluid from its' oversized body into the wings. Slowly, it continues its' metamorphosis, until it's ready to fly off. It does so, unceremoniously. Poof. In an instant, it flutters into the air, its' transformation complete.

37

The demon cums hard. Watching this human fitfully sleep, knowing it is itself fucking with him, that put him in this state. That thought caused the demon to orgasm for the first time in years. It is proud of itself. Standing there, it breaths on the sleeping figure. Last year's decaying flesh, still in its' teeth, producing a wind of the vilest kind. Death is a smell familiar with all warriors, sure to cause images to flash. Images long ago stored away, in tiny little boxes. Safe.

The demon hates safe. It inhales deep, and expels more smells of iron, of burning hair, of rotten sauerkraut, and a lifetime of battles. This demon specializes in torturing warriors. Thrives off of it. They, of the noblest kind, full of blinders, they're easy prey, once the buttons are learned. Shame, guilt, failure, and forgotten.

"You should have died," The demon whispers on the next breath. The human shudders.

"You didn't win." A whimper from the figure on the ground. The demon will have to step up its' game. "Nobody knows." "Nobody cares."

"Fuck you," the human murmurs, in its' sleep.

185

"You didn't save anybody. Not even you," the demon says, leaving. Deciding to visit again, later tonight.

Out in the world, there are many warriors to visit. Some still in training, others old and gray. Each carries the weight of old trauma. Some a lot, some a little. Who knows why some carry more than most. The demon doesn't care. It fucks with them all. Encouraging the bad, while discouraging the good. Fuck these fuckers. A couple of hours later, high on death, the demon returns.

I feel the demon's presence. It looms above me. The darkness that comes just before, reminds me of a hot-box, not the awesome horny kind, but, the kind they lock you up in, to torture you. The kind we did in P.O.W. school, the kind real P.O.W.'s had to deal with, when this is a job reality, it's good to know your own weaknesses. It helps to build them into strengths. I freaked in the hot-box, the first time. The second time was easy. Limitation faced, I grew stronger.

Stifling is the air, non-moving, it smells like socks that adorned a teenager's feet for a year, and fear, and piss. Long ago infected wounds are felt once again, the warm skin, the pus and swelling are brought to my brains memory again. The feeling of helplessness overwhelms my thoughts. I can do nothing about it. I have survived the box. Broke inside it. Moved on from that. Emerged victorious. Yet, I cannot remember that feeling. That strength.

"That's because you suck!" the demon reminds me. "You got lucky. The others were supposed to survive. You cheated. You must die also."

I open my eyes, seeing nothing. I blink a few times. The

demon's essence is so grand, no light reaches my eyes. I smell it, yet, cannot see its' form. It is strong tonight. Well fed.

"Kill yourself," the demons says. I shake my head.

"Do it," it commands me. Again, I shake my head. This is a new tactic by the demon. It thinks I will do it. "It will serve the world. Bring back balance. You upended it by surviving. You don't deserve to be here," the demon hisses.

"NO!" I yell.

"You end yourself."

"I will not quit!" I say, head in my hands, shaking it still.

"You quit years ago, the moment you moved out here. You just haven't finished it yet. You don't have the balls," the demon informs.

"FUCK YOU!" I yell, rising to my feet, freeing myself from my bedroll, I fling sand in all directions. I yell and scream, raging and thoughtless. Picking up a piece of firewood, I swing it about. Trying to find the demon through the darkness. I know it is there, yet, I cannot make contact with it. A large evil cackling sound fills the alcove, bouncing outwards into the canyon.

Reverberating.

Panting, I stand and cry. Shoulders forward, chin to chest. I weep. Eventually I sit, back to the rock, facing the open canyon before me. Shaking.

The demon visits twice more, before daylight.

38

There she is again. Closer this time. She's moving from pinnacle to pinnacle in this area of the canyon, this time she's only about 75 yards away. She's standing tall, almost as Superwoman would, hands on hips, and looking off into the distance, like she's thinking about something. Perhaps she is, perhaps she's just looking at the view from different perspectives. I recognized her the moment I saw her, even from a far distance, she's the cliff jumping nurse. Cleaned up and carrying a decent sized pack this time, she's standing there, hands on her hips, and staring off into never-never-land. Suddenly, she turns and faces in my direction. I freeze. If I can see her, she can see me. Playing rabbit, I know I'm in a decent position, purely out of habit. I forgot my bearing and did not hide from her, just stopped in my tracks, assumed the ready position, and watched her do her Superwoman impression. She is indeed, just standing there, with her hands on her hips, and basically, staring off into the distance. Or, wait, perhaps her lips are moving.

She stands on her 4th and final spire for the day. If she doesn't see him, or he doesn't appear soon, she'll have to head out of here. Her shift starts in about 4 hours and she'll have to get cleaned up before then. She can't pull a 12, after hiking all day, without getting the dust off first. It's OK to look like sweaty Hell at the end of a 12 hour ER shift, but, not when she walks in the door.

Shifting the heavier, bigger pack around on her shoulders, she laments putting the extra gallon of water at the top of her pack, instead of further down in a balanced carrying position. Putting it on top, made her top heavy. She turns to face the cliff she fell off of the other day. Scanning around with her eyes, she tries to spot him. All she sees are a spattering of huge limestone rocks that have fallen from higher above, and a myriad of sandstone rocks, halfway between cliff size and the single grains of sand below.

"Come on, come on, come on," she says to herself, over and over, "Come out, I won't hurt cha."

She had asked around a bit, trying to lightly gather some information on the people living in the forest, gather local lore, and some more detailed info from friends of hers, that are avid back country people. There's apparently more than one, rumored to live out here. Albeit a bit illegally. A couple of people she knows, said they have seen one matching the description she had given them. They have seen him in town at the local grocery, getting supplies.

Others have seen him walking down the street, or paralleling a road out in the forest. No-one has seen him out of town, except her, that is. When they all see him, they say he's heading out the west side of town, when he heads into the forest. So, it might be her guy they're talking about. She scans the cliff side and huffs. He could be right there looking at her, and she would never find him. I'll have to try something different, she thinks to herself. She pulls the heavy pack off her back and proceeds to unclip the top pack portion of it. She moves what little personal supplies she has, into the zipper area encompassing the entire lid. The lid has a simple belt system, which she uses to wrap the lid-turned-hip-bag, around her waist. Clipping the belt, she stands up and takes one more look around the canyon. Somehow, she knows he's watching her, and wants to give him one more chance. Nothing happens and she descends from the pillar, time to go get cleaned up.

I watch her work her way out of the canyon and to her car, parked in the dirt U.S. Forest Service parking lot. After working my way up, then towards the front of the giant butte I call home, I'm able to watch her throw her pack lid into the back of her ancient jeep Cherokee and switch out her boots, into some other shoes. I can't quite see from here, but, I'm betting they're some kind of recovery shoe. Good, and she's a jeep girl, also.

I do not know why I will do it, but, for some reason, I know the next time she returns to my part of the world, I will show myself. I also know she will come back.

39

The Flicker calls to me. Calls, and calls, and calls...,
everywhere I go, I hear them. This flicker has a story to
tell me, I chose not to hear. He's relentless in his pursuit of
me, there's not a season that he's not talking to me: winter,
spring, summer, fall, he follows me about. As I migrate up
and down the plateau with the seasons, he migrates with
me. It cannot be a coincidence, can it? There's no such
thing, is there?

40

She returns on a glorious day! A multitude of thick puffy clouds are taking over the bright desert skies. The day, sure to bring temps around 90 unless graced with rain, is perfection for this time of year.

I've spent a lot of time gazing off the front of the sculpted red butte, watching for her Cherokee to drive around the bend. I've had a flexible schedule for years now, and this is how I am choosing to spend most of my evenings, as of late. The views from here are gracious, I tell myself as I sit there, repetitively, first every few days, and then every other day; it smoothed into an evening routine, within a 14 day time frame.

All in all, it was a 17 day stretch between her visits to the canyon. She has another pack with her, this one surely a used pack, just like the last one. It too, is probably full of survival bars, dry food goods, and perhaps more shaving cream and a razor. I have yet to find a use for the shaving cream, the razor actually came in handy, after I disassembled it; a finite blade edge is hard to maintain out here. Occasionally, I find obsidian brought here by humans from the high peaks, 40 miles away, up to a thousand years before I found the shards in the dirt. They were of great use for working fine cuts on cordage, animals, etc., but, were easily broken and lost, just like the half-made arrowhead I found a while ago. The flimsy razors too, had a short lifespan.

The pack she left, became a hauler of wood, and the extra straps and assorted bullshit around the shove-it pouch was transformed into other things. I'm grateful she left me these things. I was surviving just fine without them, yet, the gratitude I feel toward her is immense. She gives a fuck about me, I haven't been so good at giving a fuck about myself.

I work my way to a cliff edge that will put me in her path, it is also a position that she will see me, long before she gets close. I don't want to startle her.

She rounds the corner of the local scramble trail, feeling the elevation slightly, after her couple of weeks spent at sea level in the Hawaiian Islands. She pauses for a moment, to catch her wind. When she looks up to scout the route, she sees him. He looks as ragged as before, maybe a little cleaner, probably not. If he is there, he is waiting for me, she thinks to herself. No doubt about it.

She smiles at him and he nods his head a couple of times in greeting. She waves at him as a child would greet her favorite character at a theme park. He raises a couple of his fingers in reply.

Undeterred, knowing she's doing the right thing, she resumes her accent of the hillside. After a few moments, she's close enough to get a better look at him. Although she might be imagining it, he seems different somehow, hopeful perhaps. Moving faster than her lungs are happy with, it's a few moments after reaching him, before she can manages to say, "Hi."

He smirks and says, "Hey."

Her chest cavity heaves as she gains her breath, it must be the two weeks in Hawaii, she tells herself. "How are you?" she manages to ask.

"Couldn't be better. Are you OK?" he asks.

She smirks, "Yes, I'm OK. I just, I... returned from Hawaii."

"Hawaii? Nice! I've never been there. One of just a couple of states, Hawaii and North Dakota, I believe. How is it there?"

"It's awesome. This is my third time there. I, I go every year," she says.

The conversation reaches the awkward silence stage of every stranger's conversation with each other, the make or break point. The sun retreats behind a cloud, they're thickening, and perhaps it will rain today, after all. The breeze is slight and fresh. A canyon wren sings its' descending notes, peaceful and lonely at the same time. Her breath returns to normal.

"Well, cool," I say finally.

I look at her, standing below me on the scramble trail. She stands vulnerable and strong, ready for whatever today brings. She has this hero gene. I see it as clearly as I saw her stand on top of the sandstone tower that day, hands on her hips.

"I know a good view, want to sit and chat for a bit?" I ask, knowing the answer.

"Yes, absolutely. I brought lunch," she says, patting her pack.

"That's a good deal, a view for a lunch. Let's go," I say.

We walk the short distance to my vigilance view in

silence, it will be cool to share it with her.   The single file trail allows little interaction, and I instantly fall back into my *"I have lived alone forever mode"*, where I walk in silence, listening to the spaces between the silences, while running continuous dialog in my head.

As he leads the way to a view, she is amazed. She knew today was the day, somehow. Perhaps it was the optimism brought on by two weeks away from the trauma and drama of the Emergency Room. She loves her career, even though she needs breaks from it. When she goes to Hawaii, she stays in a small town, full of mostly locals, a distance away from the hustle and bustle of the touristy areas. It is not so much about cost savings, as it is to save herself from having to deal with drama, or trauma, while on vacation. She eats at the local places, and loves to get into conversations with those that live in the towns. Most folks are happy to interact with a tourist who treats them as equals, instead of a local attraction.

She follows him, wondering what to say. Realizing she's been watching his feet and her foot placement, as well, she works her view up from the ground. She sees lithe, strong calves, sinew from years of walking, tan, dusty from the dry sand. The ligaments behind his knees bring her to the edge of his shorts, they appear to be hand sewn. He can sew! Or at least, repair and fix his own clothes. Perhaps the lower sections of the ripstop cloth finally gave way to the acacia thorns, manzanita daggers and cacti needles, or he adapted random pants he found, or was given. Who knows? She can't help, but, notice his hikers butt, loving a good tight ass on a man.

From there, a few inches of loose shirt, before she sees his ancient, yet, still good and strong, military-style pack.

It is there as most women carry a purse, there without fault or notice, unless it's not there, then a feeling of panic ensues, until it is located. She brings her view finally to the back of his neck and the boonie hat that covers the rest of his head.

He seems to stiffen for a second, then relax again, as her view encroaches this area. Perhaps she's staring a little too hard. He's a person living in the woods, his senses are on high alert. She also thinks there's some military history in there, is sure, in fact.

I'm removed from my normal trance when I feel eyes upon the back of me. It takes a flurry of thoughts to prevent me from turning suddenly in a quick, defensive, ready to attack position. That flurry of thoughts reminding me that this woman is behind me, and I'm taking her to the very spot where I've been waiting and watching for her arrival. Still yet to admit it. When we arrive, we sit on some rock seats laid out with admiration of the view in mind. As we settle in, she breaks out lunch from her pack. Well, more accurately, the implements to make a lunch. A backpacker's stove is produced, along with a lightweight pan and what looks like tuna sandwich fixings. Wow! She went all out. I must be nodding my head in accolades, because she says, "Well, there's no reason to suffer needlessly. Save that for the times when it's mandatory."

Ouch, I think to myself.

She continues, "On today's menu at this dining establishment, we will be serving up tuna melts, along with this amazing view (she Vanna White's her arm, accentuating the view). We have tuna, organic mayonnaise, relish, and gluten free bread. I didn't know if you could eat bread, so I brought gluten free."

Resisting the urge to ask her what the fucking difference is, I say, "Sounds great Ma'am. I'll take two."

"Coming right up," she replies, as she reaches into her pack for a piece de resistance', butter. "Oh, and not Ma'am. Miss if you must, but, I prefer Angela."

Of course, that is her name. I look at my hand for a second, knowing already that it's dirty. She reads my mind and brushing some bread crumbs off of hers, juts her hand out towards me in a confident handshake move. I watch my hand go to hers, a dirty hand moving towards a strong petite woman's hand. The hands embrace, confusion and elation mix, running energies back and forth from my body to my arm and back. The handshake, firm and confident, lasts but a moment. A moment that took years to produce, and will last forever.

The smell of grilling bread and melted butter enters my nostrils. I am Pavlov's dog, in an instant. A moment of tears is fought back into the depths, and I breath deep involuntarily, ingesting the smells of comfort into my senses. My eyes close as I do this.

Angela prepares the first toasted tuna sandwich quickly and efficiently. She's done this before. This is one of her favorite things to do, while on long exploratory day hikes. She isn't doing this just for him. Angela's doing this for herself, as well. Not just for the glorious taste that will hit her lips momentarily, but, so that he knows he can have the small luxuries that life has to offer. This is what she and her dad came up with, during their talk about this very kind of moment, like the one that is currently happening. First, she had to get him through the over-protective Marine dad moments, and then, when Dad realized the daughter he raised is going to do exactly as she was raised to do: do what feels right, and is right, he suggested bringing the homeless man some type of basic creature comfort, and she figured what could be better than her self-indulgent, back country, hot food, and coffee. Oh!

She almost forgot the hot coffee, in the vacuum flask.

Angela plates the sandwich and looks up at the man sharing his view with her. It is then that she realizes his eyes are closed, and he appears to be savoring the scents wafting his way. At least, that's what it looks like, as he breaths deep, in a mini trance, with his nose working the air currents. She turns away to remove the coffee flask from the pack and when she turns back, he's looking at her. Bewildered, is the look that escapes his eyes when she looks back at him.

"Coffee?" Angela asks.

"Yes, please," he replies. He reaches out and grabs the sandwich and a handkerchief she rested it on. She utilizes both hands to pour him a cup of, still steamy, coffee. Hot and dark black, just the way her dad preferred. She places the coffee on the ground in front of him and proceeds to make her own first tuna melt.

Moist, gooey, crunchy, butter-infused goodness. The tongue rejoices. **Hala-fuckin-luyah!** Oh, my god! Salt. Fatty goodness. The scents of chicory, earth, steam, and memories, hit his nostrils. He opens his eyes and pauses his devouring of the tuna melt, long enough to sip the hot coffee. Deep and dark are the coffee's secrets, buried for a long time, it gives its' essence slowly; earth, roots, wood and seed.

41

Somewhere during the second round of tuna melts, the conversation starts, very light and surface at first. By the second cup of coffee, they turn to the 'no-holds-barred-type' of a searching conversation of two people getting to know each other, for real. Not having the luxury of many meetings, and feeling a strange comfort with each other, a container of safety is created around them.

I start talking. The most I've said to a fellow human in years, was thanks, or excuse me. Now, after a few moments of reminding my tongue how to converse, I let it out. Not all of it. But still, enough to tell Angela *(of course that is her name)* how I came to be living out in these wilds, for the last couple of years. She tells me some of her story, as well as, her dad's story. Somehow, in the midst of all that, she comes to a point where she feels confident enough to call bullshit on my story.

As they finish up the best lunch he's had in, well, forever. Angela asks him her main question, "So, why?"

"Why what?" he asks in return.

"Why do you think you deserve to live out here?"

199

Angela asks.

"Why do you think living out here is a bad thing?" I retort.

She laughs, "Living out here is not a bad thing. Hiding is a bad thing, though. Are you happy out here?"

"Yes."

"Why?"

"Because I'm left alone."

"OK. Why else?"

"I can think out here. I like being out here with the wild animals."

"Why?"

"They make sense to me. If two birds are fighting, it's because one of them is trying to steal something from the other, a nest, their eggs, or their spouse. If a mountain lion leaps onto a deer, it's because that deer is for dinner. If a deer runs, it's for survival. The animals move with the seasons, ebb and flow with the seasons, react to what the earth provides them," I reply.

"Sounds cool. But, what are you saying? Are you saying that something else doesn't?"

"Exactly, that is exactly what I'm saying."

"Well, then, what is that something?" Angela asks.

He looks at her, knowing he will come across as crazy. How could he not be taken as such? Fuck it. What does he have to lose? She'll just look at him weird, or argue, or she'll disappear and never come back again, regardless. But, he doesn't want her to disappear. He wants her to help bring him home.

"Because humans aren't like that."

"We're not?"

"No, we are not! We used to be, but, now we're not.

We're advanced enough to not have to do shit like that. We're smart enough to not have to compete. To not have to steal from each other. To not war with each other. To not... well, to not work together. We're old and outdated. We no longer need to compete for resources, and money, and yet, we still do. In fact, it's so innate in us, that those that are more aware, and yet, still evil, take advantage of such a strong instinct. It's how they get us to kill each other, like how they get us to compete for the trip to the Caribbean Islands. Giving up months of family time, in order to gain the prize of taking them on vacation for a week, and while there, spending the entire time wondering what we can do next, in order to win another vacation."

"Instead of enjoying the one we're on," she adds. Angela knows this is, at the least, partially true for her, because after the first week of vacation, she starts thinking about having to go back to work. And then starts planning her next trip, before she's even done with the one she's on. Instead of enjoying the one she's on!

"There are piles of food surplus in some areas of the U.S., in other areas of the United States, kids starve to death. In Africa, children, men and women, slave for diamonds, which they will never see the riches from. In South America, they kill each other to compete for the drug trade or power, over the other person attempting to be in power. Both sides killing the innocents they should be protecting. The list goes on. We occasionally suck a huge part of the planet into a war, because of either hatred, or resources, perceived to be needed," he says.

"So, when you're around humans, this is what you think about?" she asks.

He nods his head, shamefully.

"What about when you're out here? What do you think about?"

"I think a lot less, I watch animals do their thing. Sometimes I watch humans from a distance."

"Do you judge those humans? I mean do you wonder what evil things they do?"

"No, I don't actually. I watch them walk, I judge them for their skill levels, and for their clothes. I watch them in wonder, as they cover ground, either in a hurry to cover some more, or as they stroll along watching the wildlife. I watch them explore the ruins and the pictures left behind by the ancients. I like to see them be at peace and wonder why a species so able to be at peace, is unable to be that way, when they're not out here."

She takes a risk, deciding that since he is fed and talking, she might as well give it a shot. "Why are you unable to be that way, when you're not out here?"

He looks at her. She looks at him back. He sees empathy in her eyes. The empathy of a caregiver, of one with a different kind of hero gene. Not the one that will kill, the kind that wants to save.

Fuck it, he thinks. He sees her stiffen. She thinks he's going to run. Quite the opposite.

"Because then I'm reminded of the evil that we do to each other. I'm reminded that not all humans are good. At least half, are not... I'm reminded that none, think like I do. None! I'm the only one that wonders why we do what we do to each other. I'm the only one that knows we can be different. I am the one."

She does the strangest thing. Angela mocks him. Not through voice, or by repeating his sentences, she does it through action. Angela is sitting cross legged, what in the

70's and early 80's we called Indian style. Lower legs crossed, the right foot tucked under the left thigh and the left tucked under the right thigh. Some consider this a yoga position, others just consider it sitting. She puts down the stuff in her hands and bows down in front of him. Her chest leans forward over her crossed legs and she stretches her arms out straight in front of her. Placing her palms flat all the way to the ground, she says, "Thank you, oh, wise master. Thank you for your words of wisdom. I am eternally grateful for your time and words. I see that you have obtained enlightenment, and are reaching god status. I oblige, and ask how many members of my family shall I sacrifice, to prove my dedication and love to you, oh, wise one. Oh, god of gods."

At first, she has a serious look on her face, then a grin, slow to escape, reaches her lips and spreads, as she laughs out loud. She continues her banter, making eye contact the entire time. At first, Angela sees anger in his eyes, then bewilderment. She continues, "I see you are angry, oh, god of gods, whatever shall I do to remove this anger. Shall I keep bowing down to you, 'til you get my message. Oh, excuse me, until I get your message. Please save me from myself. You are a god. You are a god."

When the bewildered look gets deeper, she changes her tactics.......

"Your belief is the only way. Your mind is correct. We all are scum, and are unable to think anything. We're only acting on instinct, we only function through your power. What type of god are you? Are you omnipotent, all knowing? Or are you an angry god that punishes his followers? I bow down to you either way, oh, wisest of wise ones."

Still not getting the look she's hoping for, she attempts another, ...

"I hunger for your anger and grief and sadness. I know that once I dive deep down into the demons of my soul, I will find what I'm looking for...." She continues to bow in front of him.   At no point does he understand, and at no point does this deter her. "Please, oh, please.   Expand on my wisdom with your dark thoughts," she continues.

Finally, he shakes his head. Deciding to play along, he says, "Why do you want my dark thoughts?"

"I do not master."

"You don't?"

"I do not master," she says, continuing to bow slowly up and down, her back stretches as she alternates between reaching her arms towards the sky and stretching them out between them.

"Then, what is it you seek?"

"I do not seek it," she says.

"Why not?" he asks.

"Because I have found it, ol' wise one."

"Is it me?" he asks, regretting it.

She grins, keeping her teeth clenched, she fights the grin, while adding a shaking of her head to the mix. "Oh no.   No, no, no.   Old wise one."

He doesn't want to ask the question, but, he does anyway, "What did you find, what is it?"

"It is something you seek master."

"If I am the master, how is it I still seek it?"

She pauses her motions, and shrugs her shoulders, "It's just the way it works," she says.

A flash of anger crosses his eyes again. The warrior comes to the surface for an instant, and then, even that part of him realizes it is unnecessary. A multitude of thoughts rush through his head, how can he be missing it?

She continues her bowing motions, this time, with a smile on her face. Not just on her face, but, in her eyes, as well. Her smile does not look like a grimace, as his feels to him. Her smile does not seem forced. "Tell me."

"Oh, wise one, how could I be egotistical enough to believe I can help you? Oh, wise one. How?" Angela says.

Air forces its' way from his lungs through his nostrils and out, in a form of knowing.

"You are the wise one master, how am I to tell you?" she says.

This time he shakes his head.

"How is it I can tell you anything? Oh, wise one," Angela continues. "You know all, and are omnipotent," Angela continues to bow, as a smile expands.

After a pause, he says, "Please tell me. I want to know."

Angela continues her motions, "Are you sure, oh, wise one?" she asks, while bowing slowly now. The smile and joy escaping her body.

"It is simple, oh, guru of gurus," Angela sits up straight. Her back arced for posture, her chest juts out and her stomach comes in. In this moment, he realizes what great shape she's in. She radiates beauty, and something else. He can't quite put his finger on it.

Angela sits. She makes eye contact with the wounded man in front of her. She can now see his concern. Not for her, but, for himself, and what he's missing. She says nothing. Instead, she brings all the joy and laughter she has in her, all her laughter from yesterday and the day before, all the way back to her first laughter, in her young childhood. She brings it all to the surface, and shows it to him. She radiates it.

He watches her. She sits in silence, not yet answering. Yet, no longer fucking with him, if she ever was. He sees something he doesn't recognize. It radiates from her. Maybe? No, it's not that.   How could it be that. Doesn't she know of the death and destruction that exists in the world? Doesn't she know of the carnage, of the genocide, of the betrayals for greed and lust. Doesn't she know all of this?

She does. She has talked of it. She has heard of his, she's heard her Dad's stories, she works in an emergency room and sees lots of death and violence. Not all who come through her rooms are victims of their own recklessness. Many are victims of others' violent acts, and acts of depraved indifference. She knows the evil that humans do.

Yet, he sees it in her. He sees it coming out of her. Angela is showing him what it is he needs to see, and experience. What he needs to feel. The light around her is bright. The glow reaches outward from the spire they're now embossed on, and encompasses the entire canyon. Somehow, he sees it. He sees the feeling that she's feeling, it irradiates dark. It glows over fear. He laughs.

Out loud. For the first time in his entire life, it feels like, there is something different being presented to him. A grin permeates his face.

Angela sees his teeth for the first time. They need some work, but, are in decent shape for someone who's living in the wilds. He must brush them somehow.

"Wow, you do have teeth," Angela says. Sitting straight with the earth now, legs still crossed, she beams with pride, while he quickly turns crimson, such is his embarrassment.

"They look great. I mean, how do you brush them, do you do the bushman thing?" Angela asks.

"The what?"

"The bushman thing, where you take a twig and roughen it, so it looks like a witch's broom, and then..." she makes a brushing her teeth motion, with her empty hand.

Grinning still, he says, "Something like that."

"Well, then, tell, me!" she exasperates.

"I get toothbrushes in town," he says.

The grin hurts his face, while she laughs along with him.

What is this he's feeling?

"Dude," she says.

"You just called me, dude," he replies.

"Dude again."

"I used to have a friend who would say, "Dude, man, dude," all the time. It was funny as hell. We even picked on him awhile, for doing it. Then, next thing we knew, our whole crowd was saying it. It wasn't until one of us was out and about with a different crowd that any of us noticed. It was pretty funny," he says.

Mostly, she's thinking, wow, he just told a story. The rest of her is trying to figure out how she can work, "Dude, man, dude," into their conversation, within the next ten minutes.

The conversation pauses as the clouds thicken. The air smells metallic, the sun hides behind the monsoon clouds, and the static builds. They both soak in the view, and the moments of today. He is feeling the connection, the first he's allowed. She feels gratitude, because he's trusting her, and decides to go for the gusto.

"When did you learn to not experience joy?" Angela asks.

He speaks deep truth to her, "I learned that the downs came, right after the really good moments. I learned that evil is real. People really can treat each other as meat to buy, sell, consume, or throwaway, at will. After a couple of really great moments that were post-ceded by tragedy, I learned that if I experience pure joy, death will follow. Yin and yang to the extreme. So, I stopped feeling. I stopped allowing the highs, the joy."

"You stopped living," Angela says looking grateful, that he's speaking his truth.

He looks at her. "It is true, dying would have been easier."

"Yeah, and that's what Marines are known for, taking the easy way out," Angela says, with sarcasm to its' core.

"Exactly. I'm still a bad-ass, I can still do anything. (He points around them) I've lived out here for years, and could do it forever."

"Except you don't want to," she says.

"Must you call me on everything?" he asks.

"You would do the same to me, if I was waxing poetic bullshit, instead of speaking the truth as I see it. I see you bullshitting me, but, not yourself. You know part of you is dead, or still over there, or however they say it. You aren't all the way home yet, and you, of all people deserve it. Deserve to be all the way home, that is. And only you and the tapes in your head, are preventing it. Perhaps it's time to slay that final demon," she says.

How did she know, of his plans? He's prepping materials for the demon's return; ready, willing, and able to kill his ass and move on. "I am ready," he hears himself saying.

"Ready for what? Not love, that's for sure," Angela says, blasting any hopes before they arrive.

He laughs this time. "No, definitely not that. Not even close. Let's start with smiling and laughing, before even thinking about attempting a relationship with another human."

"Perhaps start with a plant?" she offers. He looks at her, inquisitively. "Yes, a plant, I think that's what they say, after recovery. They say to start with a plant and work up to a cat or dog, and go from there. No humans for a year. And you, sir, are in recovery. Self-imposed, isolated, recovery," Angela puts it to him straight.

Appreciated, the comments are, and for some reason he has no issue taking it from her. He wants her to say these things, longs for it. Has waited for it, for weeks. He knew as soon as he saw her, that she was his angel. Knew so much, that when she told him her name, finally, it didn't even register. She was already his angel. Mostly, because she knows he has to do it by himself. He just needed a reason. And finally, he has one. Not her, in case you're wondering.

"Are you good at jokes?" he asks, after just a moment of silence.

Angela smirks, "No, not even close. I'm better off the cuff, wit and humor kind of thing. Why?"

"I'm new at this laughter thing. I'm sore in the face already, and well, you know us Marines. We like to push the limits," he says.

"Dude, man, dude," she says, while tilting her head and giving him a *'what the fuck, we talked about this'* kinda goofy look. Laughter fills the air.

"Oh, you are quick."
"Told you," she says.

42

She took a risk and brought a joint with her today. After talking with her girlfriends, they figured, why not. Alcohol, no! Alcohol is an inflamer, it can bring out the worst in people. Especially ones with possible anger issues. (*"Possible?"* One of 'em said, *"We all have anger!"*) most people do, actually. Which is why her one friend, Lucy, can never find a keeper, she does all her hunting in bars, and she hates bars, she just does it 'cause that's how her mom met her dad and that turned out alright. Not.

He sits and watches as she goes through her stuff. Her backpack has all the organization of a kid's toy chest. She uses a 'shove-it pack' with an opening at the top only, and apparently, takes it literally. To her credit, many of the smaller items are zip-locked together, just not in any logical order, or organizational logic, at least, that he can tell.

"How do you find anything?" he asks, "If you need to blow your nose, do you just reach into the pack and pull out random things, until you get lucky?"

She laughs, "Yes, actually. Unless I'm desperate, and then I just..." she mock wipes her nose with her sleeve.

She apparently finds what she's looking for and reaches in, pulling out a hard case. Clicking it open, she looks around at what's inside. It is strongly organized unlike the rest of her pack. From here, he can see amber sunglasses, keys, driver's license, stuff like that. She pulls out lip gloss, and places it behind her ear. Mesmerized by this action, he watches her hand on zoom; the trimmed finger nails, free of cuticles or nail polish are taken care of, and in a low maintenance condition. The hair is pulled back, long and brown, its' sheen reflects the light of the sun and causes an amber similar to those rainy-day sunglasses he just saw in her case.

He gets lost in it. Long straight hair, a little longer than her shoulders, is flipped back behind her ear, dainty and cute it is. He feels this rush through his system, that surge of attraction. Chest thumps. His eyes dilate. Adrenaline pumps. Suddenly aware he's not as in control as he likes to be, he feels himself flush.

Her hand comes back down and he watches its' path, she pulls out some chapstick and puts the case down. Luckily, she's so into what she's doing, that she doesn't notice him watching her every move, he would feel like an idiot, if she did.

She decides to take the risk, he deserves to laugh, he needs to laugh, if she could only break through that hard, protective shell, she might get him to come back into town. She wants to save him, so badly, judges that he needs it, and wants it. She's hoping to. She draws the chapstick across her lips, lost in thought, she has no idea he's watching. Thinking of her conversation with her friends the other day, she knows her intentions are good. She genuinely likes him. It's not just that she wants to save him, not this one, at least. Really good at keeping that part of her out of her personal life, it scares her that this wounded man is finding his way into her heart. I wonder if he knows....

Putting the case down, she reaches back up, pulling the lip gloss from her ear, she plays with it in her hands. Realizing she was going to apply lip gloss over the chapstick, she feels self-conscious. Angela suddenly feels him watching her. She looks up at the lost, broken warrior looking at her, as if she were a zoo animal. His eyes are full of pain, as always, yet, curious in this moment. She picks up the little tube of chapstick and offers it to him.

He looks at it, small and white, between her fingers. Tiny and clean, her fingers are long and lithe, smooth, and inviting him to touch them. It's been so long since he's touched anything not living out here. Not making eye contact, he reaches for the chapstick and sees the contrast between her fingers and his, and it is shocking to him. His are filthy, compared to hers. He keeps a fairly clean house, yet, hers have seen soap and water, his only water and dirt to keep the yuck off of them. Dry sand is really a good scrubber, it just grinds its' own dust in, after a time. Reaching her outstretched hand, he slowly watches his come into contact with her, touching her, a shock goes through his body, she jumps, they both do!

"Sorry," he says laughing. Trying again, he slowly puts two of his fingertips around the tube and lets a few of his fingers brush against her skin. He feels the softness of them, the warmth and comfort they exude. Suddenly, he has to fight the urge to cry, he can feel the surge to his eyes.

In one calm motion, he grabs it from her hand, and

213

holding it between his thumb and forefinger, draws it and his hand back into his comfort zone.

Looking at the chapstick for a minute he brings it to his lips. It's been a long time since he's applied chapstick, or anything else along those lines. Exhaling, he enjoys a deep breath. Realizing he doesn't breath deep anymore, he takes a couple more deep breaths. Very slow and purposeful breaths, brought in powerful through his nostrils, they flair with delight, and the diaphragm fills with oxygen.

"Yo, you alright over there? You're not going to hyperventilate or anything, are you?" She smiles, "I'd hate to have to give you mouth to mouth!" and she blushes making that statement.

Luckily, he didn't notice, or he may have run off. Feeling the relax encompass his body, he indulges in a few more of those deep breaths.

"No, I just haven't been really breathing. I realized it in the moment of exhale. It felt really good to breath deep."

He hands the chapstick back to her. She places it back into the case, as she thinks a bit. She's pretty sure the surge they felt was not static. Electricity, yes, but, not from static. Suddenly fearful, she wonders if she's up for this. He is broken. Why does she think she'll be able to save him? Will it really heal her, as her therapist calls them, abandonment issues. Will saving this guy bring her dad back? NO! Of course, not. This is something else in its' entirety.

She told her therapist about her dreams, vivid and real, she communicates with her Dad. They're dreams that her therapist explains, are visions, they're subconscious conversations, based on what she knows of her Dad.

Angela doesn't care, they're interactive and healthy. She looks up from her thoughts and sees him looking intently at his hands. She watches him; he's inspecting all of his fingers it seems, when he gets to a dirty part of it, he scratches at it, rubs on it, wets a thumb with his tongue and works at it, to get it clean. She can see he has some dark dirty spots, and it's those he's working at, intently. She decides it's time to lighten the mood.

"You alright over there? Do I need to apply some first aid skills, or are you going to make it?" he looks up, suddenly self-conscious. Breaking out in a sheepish grin, he smiles ear to ear. She cannot help, but, do the same.

They talk about everything, hiking shoes, packs, where they grew up, what kind of life they had as kids. He tells her about joining the Marines at 17, the type of job he had there. None of the details, just light small talk. He's conversing with a human, for the first time in, who knows how long? It actually feels good to have her around. She feels good. Feeling goofy and relaxed, they've been sitting here relaxing for hours now. Neither of them showing signs of letting up. Then apparently, she decided to ask me the big question, "Why are you here?"

The moods break.

"I can't really tell you that. I mean I want to, well, I kinda want to tell somebody, might as well be you. You seem cool enough," he laughs, in-spite of himself. It feels good to laugh, and he's going to go with it, inspired by her. He finds the laughter cathartic. "So, I guess I will…"

He tells her, the first human being not having been there. Heck, he hasn't even spoken about it with the other men that were there. They're all alive, as far as he knows, and all could connect and converse, but, none do. It's possible they have far worse things to talk about, or, this could be the worst thing they experienced in their careers, as well, who knows? Regardless, she's sitting there staring, patiently. She waits. He tells her about that day, about his longest day. How it was his first mission, because of that, they played his song. He tells her about the waiting, and the walk, and the environment there, and he describes the Quetzal with the long tail feathers, and its' iridescence. The smells of the jungle, and the tall trees with buttresses exposed at the surface. And then, when he was done with all the light stuff, he told her the dark. The hard to tell parts, the three babies, the sounds, and smells of the genocide, our hasty exit, although he won't go into every gory detail about that. But, he does want to say how it felt, because it felt like they were running from the incident. He doesn't need to verbalize it, she knows. He can tell she can read it on his face. It's in his body, and in his being. She already knows somehow, that a huge part of him died that day, died with those 200 people. He talks about his triggers, with the sounds and the smells of certain kinds. He doesn't need to tell her that stuff, yet, it feels right.

And most importantly, she's truly listening. Not judging, she listens intently to his story, watching him squelch emotions around it, and then she listens to the worst thing she has ever been told. She had no idea. After he tells her, it is silent. She contemplates what he has said, and decides there is no time like the present to set him straight, as she sees it.

"Wow, that sucks!" Is the first thing she says after a few moments, and then chuckles.

She chuckles again, "Let me get this straight. First off, I know, that is horrific! No doubt about that," she looks at him seriously, "No doubt at all. Yet, your job, the team's job, is to go and kill them all?" she asks, knowing the answer.

"No, our job was to observe and report."

"Then, how can you say you didn't do your job? Your job was not to kill them all. Your job, was to look, observe, and leave, without the bad guys knowing you were there."

"Correct," I say.

"Then why do you feel guilty? You did your job!" she says.

"Because I didn't save them!"

"You weren't put on this earth to save them! You were put there to let others know it was going on. If you had charged down the hill, you all would be dead right now, and we wouldn't be having this conversation right now, then would we?"

"Guess not" I reply.

"Guess?"

"Yes, I guess not..."

"How many were down there?"

"About 20, that's actually decent odds for us," I say smiling.

She smirks at me, not in a nice way, but, in that "whatever" kind of way. "Let me put it this way. Here's your radio call......." She puts her thumb up to her ear and her pinky to her mouth.

"Um, breaker, breaker, one nine, over."

I struggle to maintain my mood, her antics are working. Just being around her is working.

She continues, "This is the head motherfucker in charge here."

"What do you want?" she says in an interpretation of a

217

voice on the radio.

"Um yeah, we killed them all."

"What do you mean you killed them all; you aren't even there, so, how did you do that?" her radio voice replies, indignant.

"Good question sir, well, you see, our new guy ran down the hill, and laid waste to all 20 bad guys, with his sheer will and knowledge that they're in the wrong. They just fell over like cardboard dummies, and blew away like tumbleweeds, when he approached. He is impermeable, like that."

She looks at me, raises her eyebrows, and continues, *"Did he really? That son of a...*

Well, actually, did he let the bad guys do their job first?

NO!?! What?!! Well then, I guess I need to tell the bosses that there's no genocide going on, and to continue aid then," the radio voice replies.

"Perfect! Oh, wait, what? No, they were going to kill them all, honest," she stops suddenly, "Sorry, that's not funny."

"No, no it's not," I say, through my laughter.

I can't help it, I'm sure a lot of it is not having laughed or experienced any animated joy, in years. Most of it, though, most of it is her. Watching her hold her hand to her ear and pretend to converse by radio, is hysterical. Not to mention her version of radio procedure.

She continues, "Let's try this version....

"You want to kill them all, is that right, Marine?" says her radio voice.

"Yes!"

"Your job is to observe and report!" says her radio voice.

"But, sir?!"

"I said no!"

"But, other guys get to do it."

"So, if the other guys jumped off a bridge, you would?" says the radio voice.

"Hell yeah, Sir!"

I start laughing on that one, it is so true. Well, of course, I would, I joined the Marines for the adventure.

"Better, huh. That one's better? OK, one more," she says.

Radio voice, *"Report"*

Marine on the ground, "SNAFU down here, sir."

Radio voice, *"Well, yeah..."*

Marine on the ground, "FUBAR, sir."

Radio voice, *"Of course..."*

Marine on the ground, "TGIF, sir."

Radio voice, *"What?"*

Marine on the ground, "CFI, sir."

Radio voice, *"FBI?"*

Marine on the ground, "Absolutely, sir."

Radio voice, *"Well, you guys are SHAFT. You'd better ZEGG."*

Marine on the ground, "Pardon?"

Radio voice, *"Zero excuses, getting going."*

The monsoon clouds, after building all day, tired of carrying the weight, let loose the rain, and we move under an old juniper tree for shelter.

"OK, I tried," she says, "but, it's hard to make something so very serious, funny. No matter how hard I try. I know from what little you said, that your job was to observe and to report, and that you feel it's anti-Marine to have done so, and perhaps disobeying your orders would have been anti-Marine. And what about the big picture? Would anyone have heard about it, if you guys did charge down there and kill all the bad guys, would it have made a difference then, either? I'm sure they had lots of hit squads. One just replaces another. Just like if you hadn't been there, another Marine would have been there, and instead, I would be talking to him right now. That might suck, although maybe..." the mischievous energy in her body makes her squirm. She continues, "Am I making any sense? I feel like I'm rambling on, trying to make you feel better, when it's all in your head. Or so I am told," she looks up me angrily, "I really wish you had shown yourself when I brought my therapist friend out."

"I knew it! Knew I hid from you for a reason. I would say that was pretty big of you, and presumptuous, don't you think? It would have been only the second time you met me, and you wanted to show me off to your friends and shit. I don't think so. I'm not a show!"

"That's not what I wanted to do!" she says, flabbergasted. "I wanted to help you. I just want to help you come back to society, you, and people like you, deserve it."

"People like me! What does that mean?" I say, glaring at her. She tears up and I almost feel bad.

"My Dad," she cries, "my Dad committed suicide, never really came back from his Vietnam. He killed himself, abandoning me, just after my sweet sixteen party!"

OK, now I feel bad, "I'm sorry...."

She continues, "It ruined him and he never got over his bad self." She glares at me, "Do you really think you're the only one that's gone to Hell, I mean, that has seen Hell? The bad shit that we do to each other, I see it every day!" She is getting ready to go off, "You don't see me hiding out here in the woods, throwing a pity party for myself for years!" She has a point.

"I'm sorry," is all I can come up with to say.

Wiping her nose with her sleeve, she continues, "We all have trauma and drama in our lives." She looks up to see me smiling, "Whaaat?" she says.

"You just wiped your nose with your sleeve, congratulations, you have adapted, you have overcome your aversion to using tools you already possess."

"You're on your way to thinking like a Marine. Everything is a weapon, or tool. Overcome and adapt." My smile grows as I talk.

"Whatever," she says. The smile enters her face, she's beautiful when she smiles, the hair glistens, her eyes do the same. She looks down at the ground, then looks up and grins, as she slowly draws her sleeve across her face, smiling mischievously as she does, amusement in her eyes. When she's done, there's a light wet streak from her right nostril across to her cheek bone.

I lean in, way in, and just able to reach it, wipe the wet streak off with my own dirt laden finger. Leaving a small dirt streak in place of the snot. Laughing, she wipes the remainder off.

"Point taken," I say, "...and enough said on that topic, I think. Now, how about something else, like, what do you do for fun?"

"Hike, of course. Get lost in the woods on purpose, scramble around and get to know the locals," she says.

The sun has returned, it glows and radiates heat into the sandstone, we sit in the shade of a juniper, just outside of its' reach, as an after-rain humidity fills the air. Nothing else exists as we talk the afternoon away. No other hikers exist, no cars, helicopters, emergency rooms, wars, history,

Earned innocence

or anything, other than our small bubble of shade.

43

As he walks Angela down to the main trail, he realizes just how much his face muscles, dedicated to laughing and smiling, hurt. Even parts of his core are sore. The random muscles not normally used, are complaining at his new-found joy. They're just going to have to go fuck themselves, and get used to it. All muscles can be trained, even those containing joy.

They reach the trail, or as close as he would get to it. Turning to face each other they, speak simultaneously, "Thanks for coming / It was good to see you." They laugh.

"Thanks for lunch / Thanks for joining me for lunch." Silence.

"Will I see you again?" she asks. He nods his head, he is sure of it.

"You'll be different next time. I see it. It's a good thing. Good night, Marine."

"Goodnight, nurse Angel."

She smirks at that, as she takes strides down the trail. It

will be near dark when she reaches her jeep, and no worries anyway, she knows he'll be watching her until her headlights disappear over the far hill.

44

Angela drives away, realizing she never broke out that joint, and smiles.

45

I hurry to my vista point, after she disappears around the first corner of the trail. The clouds return as I watch her walk the entire distance to her jeep, watch her drive out of the dirt lot, and watch as her headlights lead her over the far hill. The strange cloud cover allows me to see her headlights as they bounce the light at every hill she crests, until even they are too far to be seen. Before I know it, it's two hours later, and way beyond dark. Time to prepare myself, tonight is the night. I will it so.

46

I awaken from the light sleep. I smell the demon coming. The wind wafts its' scent in my direction, just a taste on the wind. The demon is good, it's always good. This time, the wind betrays it, just enough to alert me to his presence.

The rotten smells of vegetation stewing in stagnation, mixed with the sweat from ages of betrayed warriors, blood, urine, shit, stale cigarettes, failure and defeat, intertwined with death, alert my nostrils to the demon's presence. Just a slight scent, wafted in by the breeze.

The demon had stopped the wind with its' powers, yet, the times are changing, so the earth sneaks off a breeze to help this human sleeping in its' playground. I go back to sleep on the surface; my insides are humming. Focusing the energy, I calm it a bit. The demon stopped its' approach. Perhaps it feels something is not right?

The demon approaches the man it's been torturing; he's ready to be finished off. His will is broken and bent, he'll be served as a snack, for all that are present when the demon returns to its' asylum.

A hard wind is blowing as it approaches; pausing, the demon waves its' hand and the air goes completely still. The demon can't have the wind giving it away, so close to victory. Slithering its' way along the cliff-face, it drags itself along the crease between the sparse greenery and the sandstone. A tight squeeze, the demon morphs its' body, fitting the contours, absorbing and discharging objects as it moves, restoring them to their previous shapes, now tainted with the demon's essence.

The demon stops, something isn't right. Is the man awake? Is he not there? The demon's hackles are up, it pauses there, and waits for an eternity. The man feels different. Is he really asleep? Is it too late? Have I played with him for too long? Taking two quick sniffs at the air, the demon smells the delicious scent of fear that it was missing a moment ago, perhaps it was the stagnation of the wind, that prevented the scent from obtaining his nose hairs attention.

I lay there, willing myself to feel asleep to the demon, yet, it stands there, and waits. I can feel it. Waiting around the corner its' hackles are up. I can smell the demon's fear. That's it! Closing my eyes tight, I focus on things that scare me. That damn Jaws movie... nope, not working. Halloween movies, nope, not working. I think next of boot camp, and then to the pool at Recon school, any and all of my military scary moments. Damn, still not working. Nothing I can think of is bringing up the fear that the demon is used to smelling from me. I am doomed. If I don't get this fucker, I'm screwed. Then I get real, and suddenly, the possibility that I may play out the rest of my life out here, alone, enters my mind. No love, no one to care about, no one to care about me. Even me.

The demon resumes its' progress, the fear scent primary in the air, its' confidence has returned. This will be the final night with this broken warrior. The demon and its' compadres' will taste him tonight. The death and destruction that the man carries, will be honey on their tongues, the souls of the dead that he carries, will fill our bellies with nutrition. His defeated soul swells with the goodness that demon bodies desire. He will be a feast of feasts, fit for the kings of the demon's world.

I lay there shivering with fear, the realization that my sanctuary has become my coffin. I will not live the night; the demon will defeat and eat me tonight. I can feel it.

The darkness looms. The slight breeze bringing awareness, dies an evil death. The demon smites its' lackluster energy, stagnant, the air exudes decay, death, and the farts of eaten fear. The demon swells in anticipation of the energy it is about to consume.

My eyes still closed, I feel nothing, but, the demon swelling above me. The time is now.

I awaken and scream in primal fear, the sounds of attacking mountain lions, pterodactyls, and frightened little boys, intermingle in my throat. I let them gather for a moment, before I'm unleashing them again. Looking away from the demon, I scream into the alcove's center. The sounds gather in the vortex of the cavern and expels itself out into the canyon, echoing to infinity the sounds of desperation and surrender. I feel the demon inhale the power of the scream, hear its' lips part, drool hits the ground with a plop, and its' skin creaks at the effort of the rare smile.

A battle rages inside the demon, this happiness it feels whenever it's on the verge of a victory, causes a paradox of confusion every time. Happiness is its' enemy, joy, the death of it. Even the demon feels it for a moment, before consuming the joy with its' evil. The demon scours its' forehead into a mass of hatred. The eyes close until they are slits. Its' drool and snot hang intermingled, these two cannot quite let go of their tenacious grip on their host.

I lay there quivering, my back to the demon, I smell the scents of the "CS" gas and gunpowder.   Briefly, very briefly, I thought I actually felt joy, coming from the demon. It felt like the alcove brightened, and the air lifted, just for a moment. The demon thinks it has won!

Swelling to all its' size and might, the demon prepares to attack for the final time. The demon's presence fills the alcove, until it is lifting the roof, pressing the stone back and away from it. The entire rock butte creaks from the pressure of its' might.

Delighted at this victory, it reaches for the sleeping man. This man's whole essence, quivers in defeat. Pausing for one second more, the demon marvels at its' work. Breaking this man was entirely too easy, all he had to do was show him one act of evil and wait. Time, and the man's own brain did the rest.

Moving its' head back and forth, the demon cracks its' neck, the sounds of pine trees breaking, soars enthusiastically throughout the canyon. Ready to eat now, the demon inhales deeply, dirt, soot and filth enter its' lungs, they savor the breath. Standing tall, the demon puffs out its' chest and rears its' hand back, talons at the ready, the remains of other victims under his nails, cloth from their clothes, and gray matter from their brains, cake the underside of its' nails. Delightfully, fungus and disease grow there.

Willing its' claws sharp, the demon moves in for the kill. Swiftly. Squeezing itself into the alcove, it rages towards the sleeping man, the human's back is the target of teeth, his balls the right hand's goal, and the delightful brains the lefts hand's target. The man turns!

Turning, I raise a sharpened wooden spear towards the impending demon and brace the hilt against the back wall of the alcove. I hold the 6-foot spear with my entire body, tilting it toward the demon in a hurry for a kill.

Unable to stop, the demon impales itself onto the first five feet of the spear before it can cease its' forward motion. Angry, the demon arches its' back and rages its' lungs empty of pain.

"WHAT happened? This man smelled done!" The demon rages, sending spittle far off the cliff with its' outrage. Looking down, the demon smacks the end of the spear with its' hand, sending it flying out its' back and off the cliff. It sniffs, and readies itself once more. The demon charges again.

I kneel with my back to the demon, waiting. When the demon reaches maximum speed, I spin around. Pulling another spear from its' buried position in the sand, and brace it against the back wall. The pocket I carved into the stone, holds the giant spear's hilt at a perfect angle. Hopefully, the stone will be robust enough to hold under impact. I put my arm over the shaft of the spear, and grabbing on with both hands, I brace with all my might. I must aim the spear at a primary angle, aiming the tip at where a heart would be, if a demon has one.

The demon hits the spear, oblivious to its' existence. For a moment, I fear the demon will just drive its' way thru the spear, and crush me with its' elephant-sized body. Every time I see this fucker, it gets bigger, the time to defeat him is now!

Finally, just as it seems the spear will prove ineffective, I see the demon's eyes go wide. The pain extravagant enough, that even a demon cannot deny its' existence. The demon slows its' forward motion, perhaps too late. As I'm pushed against the back wall, the spear moves slightly, pinning me behind it. Unable to breathe, I fight panic, as my chest cavity is forced into the shapes around me. I wait for the all familiar sounds of breaking bones. Damn, I was so close, I almost won!

Closing my eyes, I feel myself lifted forward, the spear deeply embedded in the demon's chest, my upper body entwined with the spear, holding on with all my might, we're both brought out of the tight corner. I leave skin and hair behind. Earth, rock, and dirt come with me.

The demon roars. I hear a multitude of animals fleeing the area; they run at full speed through the forest, in the darkness of the night. The sleeping birds awaken and squawk their displeasure at the sound, as their wings frantically beat the stagnant air, trying to get a purchase on something that will remove them from the scene. Large four-legged animals scurry, leap and beat feet or hooves from the area. Bushes and limbs are pushed, broken and forcibly removed from their path. Terror creates a super strength; all flee the evil escaping the demon's lips. Shaking its' arms and body in a multitude of directions, the demon tries to dislodge its' victim's impediment from its' chest. Forgetting to use its' hands due to rage, the demon swings about recklessly.

Choosing my moment, I wait for the demon to turn in the direction of my desired flight. I hold on with all my might, as my ears whimper from the sound escaping from the demon's lips, the force of the sound, nearly pushing me off the spear, with its' rush of violence. Instead, I cling to it while the rage pushes, and the demon's body thrashes back and forth. I swing between the open air and the cliff face. Alternately, feeling the air beneath me and the brutality of the sandstone, each time I bash against it.

With the next swing, I let go of the spear. Choosing the open air off the cliff, over being bashed against the rock face one more time, I fly through the air.

Willing my body to come around and assume a chest forward, arms back position, I do my best flying squirrel imitation; a cross between a controlled fall and all out desperation. I am flung off of the cliff.

Knowing it is coming, I wait for it. The impact with the trees, that is. The demon has flung me in the perfect direction. I feel the trees coming quickly, and I brace my body for the impact. Arms and legs outstretched, ready to grab anything upon contact. There is no time like the present. In fact, now is the only time. - BAMM - I fold on impact.

Grasping for anything, I leave fingernails, blood, and skin all the way down. My goal is not to stop myself. Attempting to slow my decent, I race the demon for the gravity of the ground. Knowing he'll be behind me, I urge the gravity to hurry up. Not knowing what speed of impact is livable, I give it all I've got anyway.

Thank the gods for training; the balls of my feet hit the ground, and I instantly tuck my chin and roll off to the side. Avoidance of the knees is paramount to my survival. The force, the speed, and the dark, almost got me as I roll to the right. Hitting a scrub oak, I bust out the other side, running like a motherfucker on fire. I haul ass out from under my alcove area. Heading deeper into the canyon, running with my everything, using night vision and knowledge of my backyard, arched slightly forward, head down between the shoulders and eyes up, I move as if it is daylight. The booby traps are left and right, bullets try to go through my brain as I dodge the agave, prickly pear, and the great meat slicer known as Manzanita. The pine and juniper attempt to impale my head with sticks and take out my eyes as a bonus. I smile and run faster.

I move through the terrain; it goes from high desert to high jungle to the lowlands of a couple of coastlines. The earth turns beneath me, as I make my way to my last stand and I look forward to this battle. It is time to know, or die.

Leaping off the next ledge, I reach for my tarzan rope. In the pre-dawn light, I may be able to see its' location, about five feet off the cliff, it hangs off of a tree on the other side. Behind me, I hear branches shattering, terror flings the brush, the dirt and the rocks in all directions. I better hurry, he's catching up! I see the rope and reach for

C.M. Halstead

it, as I fly by. Grasping at it, I find a purchase and close my fingers around it. Burning is the primary sensation, as the force of motion slides my hands down the hanging rope heating them to the melting point. Knowing the knot at the end is fast approaching, I grip tight. When I reach the end of the dynamic rope, my bottom hand's palm is on the knot before I know it and the other hand tightens instinctively. The climber rope I found who knows when, is stretching with all its' might to do its' job. My body stretches out behind it and then it rebounds me into the sky. A huge dark mass covers the sky above me. Stank and spittle precede its' gross arrival. I prepare. The impact doesn't come! I feel two pieces of steal raking my leg, but, no impact.

The demon reaches for the man, stretching its' reach, it leaps over the edge, gravity is of no consequence to it. Seeing the man below, the demon floats its' way above him and then crashes itself into the earth. The impact with a rock in the soil, pushes the spear out. The demon breaths in the essence of the man's guilt, fear and shame. It feels nothing! Confused, it seeks the object of its' desire. The man is done, squished, defeated below it. Why does it not feel its' new victory? The demon lays in wait.

The rope relaxes and gravity takes over again, this time I will let go of the rope when it is done lengthening, and stay on the earth. When I reach the earth, I find the demon lying face down. The spear laying nearby. He is not dead, it is not dead. Walking to the spear, I make sure to face the demon; it lays in waiting, wanting me to come within reach. I can sense it playing dead, lying in wait, it's

235

game is so obvious now. It waits until I think the demon is no longer around, no longer a threat, then it attacks. No more.

Pulling out my K-bar, I fix the tip of the spear; after shaving off the broken shatters of wood, I carve a sharp tip into the spear. In only a matter of seconds, the knife is back in its' sheath. Grasping the spear with both hands, I raise it above and behind my head, intending to use all my force, I bring it down through the demon. Malicious with intent, it breaks through ribs and sticks in its' belly. I attempt to pull it out, with intentions to use it again, and again, and again. Bouncing on it with all my weight and will, I'm able to dislodge the spear from the wounded demon's belly.

I stand before it. Panting. The demon pants, as it does, synchronicity has us heaving for breath, together still. I decide to catch mine later and plunge the spear into the demon's groin.

Withdrawing the weapon, I take a huge step forward and, swinging it around my back and down, I castrate the demon. Its' balls fall to the ground, disappearing into the earth. The demon grabs at its' groin in shock, and pain. The demon arches its' head to the sky, preparing to draw in a breath to scream, or call for help, who knows which. I don't let him; I swing the sturdy spear, baseball bat-style, severing the demon's head in a single blow.

Continuing to assault its' head with the spear, I bash, and bash, and bash, until it is mush on the ground. Dropping to my knees, I drop the spear and grab handfuls of its' brain; shoving it into my mouth, I swallow mouthfuls before my body rejects it and projects it in all directions. Unabated, I eat some more with the same results. Turning, I look for the object my body says needs to be destroyed. Spotting the hole in the ground, I move over on my knees, reaching in to withdraw the demon's scrotum. Squeezing the balls in my hands, I squeeze until they pop and throw them back into the ground. There'll be no reusing these!

Standing up, I pee on the demon, releasing any and all remaining remnants inside me, I vomit on the remains. Then vomit on it one more time, for good measure. My feet beneath me, fail to find steady ground, ankles teeter-totter back and forth. Knees bang off of each other intermittently. I loose all shape and form, and fall to the ground. Hitting hard, I inhale and exhale sand, mixed with air. I slide my face out of the ground and turn my body onto its' side, passing out with the sight of the dawn's misty light intermingling with the steaming guts of the defeated demon, the smell of its' dank innards inducing another vomit as I do. Maybe this is it. I think I did it this time.

47

I dream of turkey vultures circling above me, high in the thermals they gather, first one or two, then a few more, until they number about a dozen. In my dream, they gather their numbers before starting their slow decent. Effortless, they glide their way closer to the earth. Quickly, they're within range of the trees, and reach out with their legs to grab a tree limb.

Suddenly, an awkward screech fills the air, horrible and un-majestic, it instills fear just the same.

The vultures squawk in sudden rage! Frantically, they gather their bodies for flight, their feet frantically prance for footing, the wings shiver, the vultures shimmy into position, as they alert each other to what they already know.

A massive force swoops into their midst, yellow talons out in front, it reaches for two of the vultures, as it bangs into another with its' beak and chest. Grabbing one with a talon, the Eagle successfully knocks the other two off their perches, letting go of the captured one a brief second after it squeezes the life out of it. Turkey vultures escape in all directions. The eagle chases them into every direction, sending them to the four corners of the earth. His mission accomplished, the Eagle soars in descending circles, until he is acutely aware of his success. Shrieking in joy, he gains a perch above the sleeping human. The man, weary from battle, sleeps the sleep of sleeps, death knocking on his door, is just out of reach, as his body assumes a state of coma, for the protection of healing.

The Eagle protects the warrior from its' perch above. All being well, it preens itself. Removing the skank of the vultures from its' feathers, preening, it pulls rejected feathers from itself with its' beak and releases them to find their own resting place. One large golden feather slowly descends on the breeze, wafting peacefully, as it looks for the perfect purchase below. Seeking the object of its' desire it floats around, meandering from high to low, seeking.

The man dreams of a battle above him, violent and quick. The sun creates dots between him and it. They move around in chaos until there is only one. This one's shadow circles and circles between him and the earth's heater. Hot, cold, hot, cold, he feels until the shadow stops. He hears the sound of victory and the warrior rests, knowing it is safe.

A shadow slowly passes by from left to right, right to left, repeating this pattern as it grows. Bigger and bigger, until the shadow stops.

I awaken suddenly!

Startled to see the sky, the dirt beneath me feels alien, and familiar. Taking a very deep breath, I release it toward my chest. A big golden feather shutters, as it spins around from the breath. I reach down and pick it up, it is a large one. It seems perfect. Reality in my hand. Making motions to get up, I feel every inch of my body in pain, slowly, painfully, I raise myself to a sitting position. Now that I'm moving, I realize I'm battered. I smell like hell, death, and war. Something sticky and strange is on me, also all around me on the ground. It is as if something exploded its' guts out.

Gathering myself to my feet, I slowly stand up straight. Getting the urge, I reach for the sky, feather still in hand. Stretching with all my might, I feel taller than I remember ever feeling before. An Eagle fills the sky and it circles above me. I watch for a couple of seconds and then hear a loud screech, just before it flies off.

48

Sleeping soundly, the faint sounds of rain enter my ear channels, finding their way to the ear drums, the water plays its' song on my unconscious. Melodic, it brings me from the deepest sleep, stirring, I become conscious of its' tune. As I awaken, it strengthens. Coming down at a full roar by the time I'm fully awake, I lay there and listen for a while. I can hear the rain falling from the sky, and landing around me, it hits the cliff sides above me and bounces off, finding its' way to the ground.

The water gathers way above me, not just in the clouds, but, on the cliffs and the levels above, the water finds its' way into the low areas and gathers its' steam, slowly at first, it seems to meander its' way together, speeding up on the slopes, it creates channels in the limestone,   enhancing its' trip to the sandstone below, where it attempts to catch up to the rain already there, zipping its' way to the ground.

Gathering, it forms little streams and rivers that work their way down through each level. Every living root attempting to gather the water, as it races for the dirt below. I lay there listening to the falling water as it crashes, even weeps in some areas. In others, it meanders and flows, slowing, working its' way through the obstructions to the ground. Some finding ways into each crack the sandstone offers to it. As I lay there listening, a drop of water hits my forehead. Looking up, I see a crack in the alcove above.

"Hmm, that's new," I speak.

"Hello," I speak again. It sounds different... hmmm.

Unsure of this new sound, I decide to whistle. Testing my whistle, I gently push it from unsure lips. I stretch as I start my day's movement. Feeling light and motivated, I get up faster than usual. Before I realize it, I'm whistling loud and strong, as I go about policing up from the previous night's activities. Water drips down into my home for the first time ever, I have experienced quite a few rains over the time I've lived here, this is the first time it has entered, must be that new crack in the sandstone. Must be time to move on.

The rain comes down steady, not so thick that I can't see across the canyon, yet, heavy enough that a steady waterfall showers down from above the alcove. Feeling a strange urge, I walk over to it. Putting out my hand I feel the water, it looks clean and pure as it flows over my hand. I pull my hand out of the water, and can't help but notice the contrast between its' clean appearance and the rest of my arm. Stepping in, I feel the waterfall's chill. Ice cold, it comes from high in the desert's spring sky, cooling everything it touches. I step all the way in. The water falls onto my dirty skull and causes that freezing, pulling skin feeling that goes with the shock of the contrast.

Slowly, I turn my head up to the flow and it runs across my forehead and onto my face, as I tip it towards the sky.

Everything the water touches tingles with needles and electricity. The water, falling clean, bitterly turns brown as it works its' way down my body. Realizing its' mission, it vigorously cleans my body of the filth. Joyfully hitting the ground, mission accomplished, it uses the earth to cleanse itself of the demon's remnants.

The water continues its' journey, gravity pulling it downward, to cleanse and nourish everything in its' path.

I am sitting. Watching. The Stellar Jays are doing an outstanding job of protecting their eggs from the persistent raven. They have chased him off, several times, over the last couple of days. Someday soon though, the parents might get careless, and the raven will succeed in a luscious meal of newborns. Nothing better to do, I figured I would just sit here and watch the process. I remember how I felt when I first came out on the land, remember thinking that only humans were cruel to each other, only humans stole from each other, fed off each other. Not true. Not even close. In fact, it seems it's the lay of the land, when there's not enough to go around. Plethora is the life to strive for. Plenty for all, then there's no competition. When there's enough, there is no reason for death and destruction, no need to steal, or for thievery. It's only when there's not enough for everybody, that the way of the land kicks in. People will compete for the same resources, famine brings war, shortages of fuel brings war. Space... human territory that will support human life, is always fought for. Such is as it is in the wilds, as well. Here, nature is in full charge, she determines the cycles of life out here. Out here, it is in short cycles, whereas, in the human world, it happens on a much slower scale these days, due to the frequently logical human brain, and the technology it's capable of producing.

On wet years, there's plenty to go around, extra grasses, extra bugs, extra, extra, extra! Lots to go around, no reason to steal, no reason to kill the young, no reason to... yet, they still do. I sit here watching the raven, it perches a few feet away in the shade, on the top of a tall pinion pine, perched with its' back to the nest, pretending to pay it no mind. Back at the nest, the female and the male Stellar Jays have a chat. It's decided, one will stay and one will go. He flies off on chores unknown. She settles in, working the eggs into a perfect warming position and nests with them.

A different raven approaches, this one flies right up to the nest. The father Jay, still in the neighborhood, comes racing back and dives at it, gaining its' attention, he draws it away from the nest. Another raven comes flying up, the female Jay having an instant to decide what to do, decides instead of hunkering down and being invisible with her eggs, to fly up and lure the raven away. She does so, successfully. Squawking and fluttering her wings, she draws this raven off, away from the nest. The third one, the one we all forgot about, flies up, and triumphantly grabs all the eggs in its' beak and, unceremoniously, flies away, never to be seen again.

Or at least, until all three of them are hungry again, and feels like working this neighborhood for more eggs. Even though the third Raven was in cahoots with the other two, he might not even share the bounty with them. Such is the way of the world.

It is a wet year, there is plenty to go around. There are tall grasses to hide extra bugs that the jays can eat and produce extra eggs that the ravens can steal, to produce more young ravens that the Coopers Hawks can eat. Such is the cycle in the wet years, the time of plenty.

In the times of dry, the lean years, there's not so much of the plenty, less and less to go around, as those years back up to each other. Then, the competition becomes fierce. Instead of working together, the ravens compete and fight over eggs, and territory. The jays produce one, or none, in the egg category. They, having very few insects to eat, they, having no grass to hide in or to place their eggs on, are eaten rapidly by many near starving birds. Those that can, move north, or closer to springs, were the competition is a little less fierce. Those that can't move, go lean, if they make it at all.

In those years, the bugs of decay thrive, and they only. Then, towards the end, they give the birds sustenance in their plumpness, some fat for the winter to come. Next year it will be better.

"Come into town," was the last thing she had said to me, when she left that day. That day he laughed, for the first time in many years, was some days ago. It took him some days to get up the gumption to come in, well, that, and a last battle that had to be won.

I stand across the street, looking at the Emergency Room, the large, glowing, red letters announcing the entrance. Standing there, I watch. The traffic whizzes by, left and right just between us. An ambulance arrives, doctors and nurses come out, she is one of them. He disappears mentally, so she cannot see him. He watches it all, invisible, for the few seconds it takes them to assess, and take the patient inside.

Standing there, stone-still as traffic goes by, waiting for a gap. It seems like forever, before the traffic abides my will and creates one, so that I can cross. Crossing to the median, I prepare to wait, unnecessarily, since the traffic has decided to cooperate. Stepping foot on the curb on the ER side of the road, I feel a kick to my step, a lightness to each stride forward. Approaching the doors, I consider leaving my pack outside. I never separate myself from my pack.

Old habits die hard, and everything I've needed, since the age of seventeen, I have carried on my back. Now at 40, I don't know what I would do without it. Hunched over from the weight of the world on my atlas, I have 'turtled' my neck forwards for as long as it can remember. Reaching the shade of the great entrance, I pause for a decision, standing there in the middle of it all, I consider my options. Will I look less homeless, if I am not wearing a pack? Wait! Back in town for five minutes, and I already care what they think, screw that!

49

Nurse Jenkins, heading for a cigarette break, spots the homeless man standing outside in the middle of the unloading zone. On pause, he stands there, still and effortless, as he continues to contemplate something. He has the 1,000-yard stare in his essence. Who knows what's going through his head? Wait, this one looks like the one Angela keeps talking about, old school pack, reddish beard, his sunhat hides most of his facial features, yet, she's pretty sure, somehow, it is him. She decides to put her highly coveted cigarette break on hold.

"Hello there," she says to him, gaining his attention and smiling in his general direction. "Come on... come on in," she says, while motioning for him to come towards her.

Someone's voice rattles my focus. I see a nurse standing there, a cigarette and lighter in her hand. It's not my nurse, but, a nurse just the same. Motioning for me to come forwards with her hand she says, "Come on in." I take my left arm out of the pack strap, and with the pack slung over one shoulder, I walk toward the lady. She reminds me of Flo, from an old television show I watched as a child. She used to say things like "Kiss my grits." I can see this lady has a lot of that in her, as well. "Yes, ma'am," I say as I approach.

"Good, glad we're on the same page, I'd hate to go all charge nurse on you," she puts her hand on my shoulder, gently, and pats at it, then leads me inside the Emergency Room. Walking up to the front desk, another nurse looks up, inquisitively. She knows Nurse Jenkins will only give up her cigarette break for dire emergencies. It's out of her character to assist this homeless guy, during her smoke time. "Would you let Angela know her friend has arrived?" Turning to me, she asks, "When's the last time you had a check-up, hun?"

I crack a smile, "God only knows."

"That's what I thought." Looking back at the nurse behind the desk, "We'll put him in examining room seven." she says.

Angela approaches quickly and softly, I can feel her coming closer. She's happy and light on her feet, yet, smart enough to be cautious. Her energy stops, just outside the door. Pausing breath, I listen with all my might, gaining another ounce of information on her intentions, would be awesome right now. What can I not hear? She appears before me, her breath suddenly in front of me. Antiseptic and lavender are the smells that mix with her nerves. It takes an amazing amount of will to lift my head from the safety of the floor's gaze and her image in the shiny surface, a filtered being. Sitting back a bit, I raise my gaze, bringing the intent up to her face. The reality of her chin, imperfections in the skin, cheek twitching, and nostrils flaring, as she tries mercilessly to keep her shit together. My eyes meet her quick moving pupils, they flare and shrink as she moves them about my face, quickly refocusing. I take a risk and decide to see her eye color. I need to know, for some reason.

What a mistake... a 2x4 hits me up the side of the head, a 220-volt jolt of electricity flies through my body, ... time ceases, and nothing else matters. I am fucked now. Fear and adrenaline surge.

"Why are you here?" she says, "I mean, um..."

My brain says several things, none of them escape my lips.

"OK," she says.

"Sorry..." escapes my lips.

"For what?" she says, quietly.

"Nothing..." how do I communicate again? "I fell, it was my turn to fall."

Stepping back, Angela takes a look; somehow his face is untouched, just about everything else she can see, has either a cut or a bruise. There's even swelling in a few places.

"Oh, my god! What happened to you? You did fall, didn't you," she laughs at his nonchalance. "You fell a long way, from the looks of it. When did this happen?" she asks.

"The other day, I leapt off my cliff."

"What?... Why?" she asks.

"I had to lure the demon, lure him into a trap."

Fear shows on her face for a second, replaced by that nervous cheek twitch.

"I'm done with him, he can hurt me no more. I ...." *Tell her!* My brain is screaming. "I ate his brains, so he can't eat mine." Whew, I said it. "Three times, he's gone now."

She smells the puke on him, fresh sweat and blood, but, not that ancient musky smell that emanated from him before. She feels like that statement he just made "should" worry her, but, it doesn't. He has released something huge, intuition tells her this is truth. He was in battle once again, perhaps for the last time, this time for himself, for his soul. There was nothing anyone, but him, could do for that.

"Does this mean I get to cook your dinner?" she asks.

"Sure, how about a shower first?" I ask.

"Not so fast, Marine...." she says laughing.

Then she says, "Yes, you can use my shower, and my soap, and my everything."

I put my hand on hers, pausing her motions, making eye contact with her for a minute and thank her for everything. Not a word is spoken, and all is heard. Taking my hand back and putting it on my lap with the other one, I sit there like a good patient and let her poke, prod, measure and quantitate my body, as needed. It all gets recorded in a little chart. Based on the humming and whistling, she seems to be enjoying the process, greatly.

"*It will be OK. He will be OK*", Angela thinks to herself. He has started coming home already, she has seen lots of changes in him, over the last couple of weeks. There is hope for us.

Suddenly, an ambulance pulls up, sirens blaring and lights flashing, a police escort pulls in behind it. Lots of commotion, as the ER staff run outside into the comforting chaos; it all flows inside, noise and motion everywhere. The man on the gurney yells in pain, as they wheel him in. One of the nurses tries to get his attention, as they wheel him off.

Relaxed, I am relaxed. I can't help, but, smile, comforted by my non-reaction at that chaos. The journey home continues. Without realizing it, I slowly lean into Angela, as she works. My forehead on her belly while she deals with the wounds on the back of my head.

As Angela dresses his physical wounds, she can see he's worked on the other ones. He has changed drastically, since she first looked up and saw him, crouching in the shadows, watching her lay there after her fall. He had scared her a lot in that moment, and not because she had just fallen off of a cliff, either. He was scary looking, he had a mean set to his jaw, a scowl on his squalid face, and he was wearing the same beat up clothes he's wearing now. Except now, they're cleaner somehow, and patched up more. Someone, had to be him, sewed up all the rips and tears, any threads and strings have been trimmed off. How did he pull that off?

"How did you repair your clothes?" she asks him.

"A sewing kit is part of my field gear. I showered in the rain yesterday, and spent all night fixing my clothes."

She notices then, that he is leaning into her as she works, now with his forehead on her belly, she stops dressing his wounds and cups the nape of his neck, which he has exposed to her. Rubbing her hand gently up and down the area, she hears him sigh.

"Welcome home, Marine. Welcome home."

My forehead on her, her hand caressing, the first comforting in my memory, I fight back a tear and then say, fuck it, as I let a couple hit the floor. I let my hand reach out and touch her nurses uniform, it is rough between my two fingers. Letting go of the cloth I embrace the words she's saying, and touch the leg beneath, gently with my fingertips, the warmth comes through into my hand. Suddenly uncomfortable, I stiffen and go to sit up.

Angela says the words, not sure where they came from, just knowing they are the right ones, what he needs to hear. Feeling him stiffen and pull against her hand in an attempt to sit up she lowers her hand from the back of his head to his upper back, as he tries to sit up.

Her hand firm on my back, she presses between my shoulders, bringing me back towards her. I hear her say, "Welcome home, welcome home." Settling into it, a sigh escapes me.

"Yeah, that's it," she says.

Angela leaves for a bit and then comes back with hospital food and coffee. As I quickly consume them both, she sits quietly. She seems to be thinking, perhaps working up to saying something.

"I hope you're not upset with me," she says finally.

"Why would I be?" I ask. I feel her fear.

"Because I called the Vet's Center," she says after a moment.

I do feel anger, at first. Then, I allow myself to reach the feeling underneath that anger. I would never admit it, yet, I feel fear. "Why did you do that?" I ask.

"Because they can help you," she says.

"Yeah, how so?"

"Because they've been through it," she says.

I say nothing, as I go into my head. My favorite retreat. Wait! Retreat? Hell, we don't do that! Perhaps it is time, perhaps it will be a good thing. Although I don't tell her, I know I'm ready to do what it takes to live again.

"I have to attend to some other patients. Think about it,

please? I'll be back," Angela says, and leaves me to my thoughts.

50

I walk out of the emergency room with Angela. Near a white van that says, 'Veterans Outreach' are three people chatting and waiting, patiently. When they see Angela and me approaching, their chatter stops and they stand tall. A tall lanky middle aged man, still sporting a high and tight, albeit full of grey, steps forward first and introduces himself, "Hello, I'm John. Good to meet you, Semper-Fi," he says and then steps back.

Next is the easily identifiable Navy veteran, the tall blue hat with his ship patch adorning the front gives it away. "Larry," he says, as he shakes my hand, and makes eye contact. The third vet is a female, waiting until Larry steps back before her turn. Also making eye contact, she puts out her hand and I take it, shaking it firmly, "I'm Barbara. Army Medic."

"Hey doc," I reply.

They stand patiently, waiting. None of them say anything. They simply look at me with deep compassion and knowledge. I feel the need to break the tension, I feel it coming from me.

"If you're planning to force me into that van, you

should've brought more people," I say.

John laughs, "We aren't going to force you into the van, Devil Dog. You have to choose it. You have to want to enter the van. Are you ready to come home?" he asks.

Barbara slides open the van door, Larry, the Navy veteran climbs into the van and takes a seat.

Barbara stands by the sliding door and waits patiently. John gets into the driver's seat and starts up the van. He turns on the radio and tunes it to a classic rock station. A song I know very well, happens to be playing on the radio, the piano coming through the speakers screams at me. As do the lyrics, "...*take it to your heart, feel me in your bones...*"

Angela puts her hand in mine, squeezes it and says, "I will see you soon. I'm holding you to that dinner. Soon." She puts her hand on my shoulder as she releases my hand and walks back towards the emergency room. The radio plays a song I had long forgotten about, one of my other favorite songs. As I step into the van, the soulful piano mixes with electric guitar, "*I'm on my way, just set me free, home sweet home....*"

Barbara hears the song and smiles, as she slides the van's door closed. The guitar wails as the container seals. I am safe. Once again, surrounded by like-minded people, I haven't even had a conversation with any of them, yet, I know it.

"*I'm coming off this long and windy road,*" I sing under my breath, as John turns up the radio, so Motley Crüe can be heard, as intended. No conversation necessary, I close my eyes and listen, as the song encourages me.

51

I settle in for the view. There's nothing like visiting a favorite place that I haven't been to in a long time. I don't want to say coming home, that would imply the wrong intent in this situation, yet, it's a place that feels right, and it's here when I need it. At any time, I can come back here and remember what I've been through, not to live in the wound, but, to revisit and be reminded of how strong I am. I unsling my pack, one of those newfangled military style packs, picked up from the surplus store in old town. I knew I was in the right place, as soon as I walked in: stuff was piled everywhere, the multi-generational military gear was prevalent, the fashion-type stuff was minimal. The woman behind the piles of stun guns and survival manuals owns the place, and has for years, her name is Penny. Once she saw my Marine tattoo, it was on, and she set me up with all the best newfangled gear, whilst steering me away from the cheaper copycat stuff.

Reaching into my new pack, I pull out a couple of ham, cheese, and spinach croissants. After removing them from the foil, I devour them relentlessly, until they're both gone. It was the best one minute I've had at this view thus far.

C.M. Halstead

The flakes, semi-melted cheese and the ham flavors, mingle in my mouth as I look out toward the distant mountains. Absentmindedly, I reach into my pack and draw out the pamphlet I grabbed on my way out of the Veteran's Outreach Center. Unfolding the bright white piece of paper, I read it again:

TRACKER SCHOOL

Are you confident in the outdoors,
Self-motivated, and Independent?
Heck, do you prefer to be outside?

Call (999) 968-5483 ext. 669
(Scholarships and work trade available for Veterans)

Already knowing I'm going to apply, I put the pamphlet back into my pack and withdraw a container of water. Using my tongue, I work the remnants of the treat from my teeth and upper reaches of my inner cheeks. Next is a good swig of water, which I swish around my mouth aggressively, before it is swallowed. My palate clean, I reach inside my back and pull out a tube. Removing the cigar from the protective case, I bring it up to my nose and inhale, deep and slow, the cigar's heavy, woody spice, enters my nostrils, as I roll it back and forth, between my fingers, enjoying the feeling of the firm 60 gauge cigar. Properly stored, I relish the quality of its' construction and preservation, continuing to roll it back and forth, I absorb its' oils between my fingers.

Picking up a stick, I bring it to my nose, it smells like dirt and stick. Next, I raise the hand with the cigar to my nostrils and draw in a gentle breath, inhaling the humidity of the cigar, its' musk, and the blends of the earth rolled up inside it. Tossing the stick over my shoulder, I relish the cigar and the view. The expansive valley stretches before me. It is grandiose, and finite, at the same time. A consistent transition from one moment to the next, as my eye travels through it. The only constant I see, is the ever-changing environment.

After awhile, as I zone off into my thoughts, unconscious what my eyes are seeing, just looking through the files in my head, randomly letting my brain do what it needs to do. Meditative, I enjoy the cigar and thrive in the moment. My vision picks up movement in my periphery, it brings me out of my trance. I take a cursory glance and see a cocoon starting to move. As I stare at the cocoon, it is wriggling in slow motion. If I hadn't been zoning off, I never would have seen the movement.

Now, as I focus, I see everything, every minute detail. Focusing my attention on the awakening cocoon, I move just a little bit closer, and take a gander at it with childlike curiosity. The ashen shell moves slowly, as the pupae inside pushes against it. Slow, at first, it becomes translucent as the sun illuminates the goings on inside the cocoon. I see parts of the cocoon being pushed against, as it cracks from the efforts of the critter inside. The motion is patient, no frantic claustrophobia here. Just the slow progress of nature. The shell cracks as a being inside imparts its' will upon it. Bursting forth, it wedges and worms its' way out, pushing through the small crack until the cocoon bursts open, unable to structurally resist the transformation.

Quickly, there comes a fluttering of wings, fast and furious, the butterfly beats them, vastly swollen in the body, its' wings wrinkled and imperfect. I reach out and gingerly pluck it from its' perch on the branch. Once again, careful not to damage or leave its' legs behind somewhere clinging from instinct, I bring it closer to me and place it in my other hand. Moving back to the sunny spot, I watch the butterfly do its' thing. The sun and my palm warm it, the wings power pump the fluid from its' oversized body, into the wings. Slowly, it continues its' metamorphosis until the butterfly is ready to fly off. It does so, unceremoniously. Poof. In an instant, it flutters into the air, its' transformation complete. The sun shines through its' golden wings, it flitters about, playing with the sunlight.

I raise the cigar to my lips and drawing inwards, let the smoke fill my mouth, after I moment I exhale its' goodness, the smoke rides the wind toward the butterfly. It gasps and flutters away, the smoke in pursuit. The newly transformed being works its' way in a short circle, bypassing the fleeing smoke, it comes back to me and lands on my knee. My dark pants are warm from the spring sun, the butterfly settles in for the view and the warmth. Its' transformation complete, it basks in the glory of its' brave accomplishment.

As I sit and experience the day, I realize it is my turn. My turn to help others in need. Those veterans that came to the emergency room that day, took a risk, and stepped up to help me because they had been through their version of my story. As I finish my victory cigar, extinguish it, and disperse the tobacco into the wind, I make an oath to the canyon that protected me, while I battled my demons.

"I will do the same. I step up to help others take the risks to face their demons. I hold the container safe, so that they may come all the way home," I say.

I hear a ridiculous screech behind me. Chills rise in my spine, as I arch my back and look to the sky. A Golden Eagle leaving the canyon flies above me and out into the valley. I watch as it rides the thermals, rising in all its' glory, golden in its' light. Free.

The end.......

is the beginning.

Afterwards

Everybody thinks Marines are Arnold Schwarzenegger, and big ass mutha fos, like that. Sure, there are some of those, but, most are actually way tougher. Most look like many of the people that are around you right now, just in-shape humans, that have hearts of iron, not that they aren't human, because they are, but, because they're that tough!

I don't believe a Marine is a body, he is a heart and soul Marine. It is the gumption that gets him up the hill, willpower that keeps him treading water for three hours, enables him to force march for a couple days. Spirit, some would say. It's amazing what we can do when we have to, kinda shit.

So, when we refuse to give up, when we refuse to let go and move on, remind us, we are not there, we are home. Welcome us home. Help your Marines to become relentless in their journey home. Retreat to the front. A new battlefield, redeployment, as some would say. The battle and journey home is within us. Only an individual can choose to come home. Move on from the 'every decision is life or death' mindset... because it's not,

Earned innocence

anymore.

Welcome
Us
Home

In a report in 1999, the CEH (United nations-funded Historical Clarification Commission) reported that during their Civil War, the Guatemalan government was responsible for 93% of the human rights violations, the guerrillas only 3%.

It was such a time of chaos, that it's hard to firm up any of the details, from either side. Dead and missing, range upwards of 200,000 human beings. Exhumations of victims continue to this day.

Genocide occurs annually in the human world.

Only about 13% of U.S. adults are veterans. (That's right, that's how bad-ass you are!)

Approximately 22 United States Military Veterans, commit suicide, each and every day! Please do your part, to bring them (and yourself) home: physically and mentally.

Possible avenues include:

http://www.vetsjourneyhome.org

http://maketheconnection.net/events/ transitioning-from-service

http://veteranscrisisline.net

Another Veteran (Seriously, don't

underestimated the power of this one)

Perception

<u>Murphy's Law: what can go wrong, will go wrong.</u>

This is by no means a reason to be a pessimist in life, just the opposite, really. A ***pessimist***, in this case, would say nothing will go wrong, an ***optimist*** would say everything will go wrong, and a **realist** will say everything will go wrong, and I have a solution for it.

In the trials and tribulations of our chosen warrior lifestyle, shit happens, very frequently.
It's how we handle these trials and tribulations that differentiate us from all others.
What can go wrong, will. Have a plan for it. Don't live in fear of it, plan for it. Work towards the best, until things go wrong, then enact your disaster plan, until the problem is solved.

<u>Plan for the worst, hope for the best.</u>

Militarily speaking, this translates to "shit's gonna happen, expect it." A lot of people in the world walk around in a state of total bliss, and when an accident happens, or a flat tire, or a wrong turn, they totally and utterly freak out. If they're prepared for the reality that shit actually can happen, then when it does happen, it's less likely that it will blindside them. They'll handle it, instead of freaking out.

When putting an action plan in place, we run all the bad possibilities in order to pre-think the best possible solutions to the worst things happening. Even in civilian life, the very worst happens from time to time. In our military-life, its' a guarantee. Not an if, but a when.

After-afterwards

The warrior watches the movie play out on the screen. He is seated in a prime position in the theater. The spot with perfect sound and best view of the screen. He watches a battered man on the screen charge a fugly demon with a wooden spear, the demon already bleeding from the first one. This one sticks. The filthy man holds on, until the demon flings him off the cliff. Once there, he hits the ground running… like a motherfucker on fire. The writer's favorite line flows through the warriors head as he watches the figure on the screen run from his demon. The director's version of the final battle plays out on the screen. The warrior has no choice, but, to stand up and scream, "Get him. Kill the demon. Kill the fucker!" A large loud war cry escapes his gut, guttural and very powerful. Throaty.

"Yeah! Yeah! Yeah!" he cheers the human figure on, as it passes out after the deed is done.

The warrior turns to the audience. "Do it! Stand up and do it. Kill your demon. Throw its' power at the screen and reclaim yours. Do it now!"

The audience is stunned.

Luckily it's a home audience, and many know the warrior. They're not too surprised. The stronger ones stand and yell at the screen, expletives and accusations, all are tossed at their demon embodied on the silver screen.

With a quick flurry, most in the theater stand and do their work. They take the weight of the world off their atlas, and send it off to where it belongs: Fantasy land. For it is all, bullshit.

Power and war cries fly about the theater. Those without balls or ovaries, sit and judge, whilst those that have already done the work, stand and cheer others on. Warriors at work.

More works By C.M. Halstead

The Tripper Series: 'Trip Walk' and 'Kangal' are the first two books in this adventure, time-travel, series. Book three of the series is slated for release in 2018. In 'Trip Walk' we are introduced to a team of seven "Trippers". Trippers are the special forces of their time, so new, that no-one knows they exist, they are time-travelers by trade. Kangal, book two of the series, gives us a little more insight and another opportunity for the rookies to gain experience. Book three has us returning to "the scene of the crime" and the tripper team finds out that something is not as it seems.

Mongers: Inspired by events in modern America, this was intended to be a 5,000 word short story and blossomed. Reviewed as "prophetic" and "spot-on" 'Mongers' is a great heroes journey.

* * *

C.M. Halstead

<u>The Tracker</u>: is my first released story, it is a cool satire about over-confidence and human nature.

<u>Not eligible</u>: is a story about "justification" and how easy it is for human beings to justify their actions as the right thing to do.